Under Pegasus

By The Same Author

Plays

What Goes Around
Becoming Walt Whitman

Poetry

Echo Aonides (a collaboration)
Whispers of the Morning Tide: Poems From an Edinburgh Sketchbook
the day i sang for my lunch

Under Pegasus

David Beckman

Golden Grove Books

© 1997 by David Beckman

All rights reserved.

No part of this book may be reproduced or utilized in any form or by any means, electronic or mechanical, including photocopying, recording, or by any information retrieval systems, without prior permission in writing from the publisher.

> Inquiries should be addressed to
> Golden Grove Books
> A Division of Derrynane Press
> 348 Hartford Tpk.
> Hampton CT 06247

Published in 1997 by Golden Grove Books, a Division of Derrynane Press

Manufactured in the United States of America

Printed on acid-free paper

> Library of Congress Cataloging-in-Publication Data

Beckman, David, 1944-
   Under Pegasus : a novel / by David Beckman. -- 1st ed.
     p. cm.
   ISBN 0-9651244-1-X (alk. paper)
   1. City and town life--New York (State)--New York--Fiction.
2. Homeless persons--New York (State)--New York--Fiction.
I. Title
PS3552.E2838U53   1997
813´.54--dc21   96-52223
                                                                                 CIP

For Ann Loring

*To teach is to give.
To teach well is to give life.*

And For Sharon

*Thanks for your help,
and everything,
always*

*Le vrai amour
ne se change.*

And indeed when we meet again after many years women whom we no longer love, is there not an abyss of death between them and us, quite as much as if they were no longer of this world, since the fact that our love exists no longer makes the people that they were or the person that we were then as good as dead?

Proust, *Time Regained*

Prologue

*N*ine A.M., Grand Central Station, a few years back, before the renovation: she stands just in from Track 23, playing her flute as a river of commuters divides, flows around her, rejoins, moves on. Isolated there, an island, she wears a threadbare brown coat, a faded blue woolen cap, and cloth gloves with the fingers cut out, so she can play.

And there I stand in my Gucci loafers, Armani suit and cashmere overcoat, staring at her from forty paces, lacerated by the crisp notes and tight phrases of the Bach flute concerto, her long-ago signature piece as a concert performer. She holds the flute at a jaunty angle, and up the notes fly, nearly visible, careening off marble walls, scattering like tiny birds, cascading back down in a shower of sound.

She looks at me then, eyes like lasers above her flute; she gives a little nod and her fingers go still on the flutekeys. She lowers the instrument and walks right toward me. What can I do but stand there, as in a wicked dream, and wait? She stops in front of me. From under her cap protrudes gray hair in thin clumps, which once had been reddish brown and long and lush. Her forehead is imprinted with a stanza of deep wrinkles, which once had been exquisitely smooth. And her lips — in my memory full, sensual — are thin and cracked, and at the corners pull downward, into gray sagging cheeks.

She says: "Jack. So you've finally come."

One

*T*he day before had been among my all-time best. Jack Transit, forty-five, New York adman, creative director and partner in Greenberg Transit Fulsome, flying higher than high on the coup of the year — landing the big fish, Mercedes-Benz, taking my agency into the arena where the big boys play. Yes! We'd gotten the call after lunch; the account was ours. It would require a major new spring campaign across all media, heavy on print and broadcast. Thirty to forty million in billing for the fiscal year. The office had erupted, we spilled into hallways and each other's offices, and the party got serious by four o'clock at Frank's, an advertising bar on Forty-seventh Street. Dom Perignon was the libation of choice, Carl Greenberg and Gordon Fulsome — my partners in the business — were there of course, and our troops too, everyone who'd pitched Mercedes, worked over a six-week period of late nights fueled by sweat and caffeine, knowing this was our big chance, a war to be won for pride and booty.

The word spread and friends and competitors from other shops started coming in — we were buying — and around six my secretary, Irene, and Michelle O'Malley, an account supervisor, were dancing on a table. Sometime later I worked my way through the crowd to the payphone in the bar and called Mary.

"Guess who?" I asked.
"Where are you?"

"Partying. Ready? We got Mercedes."
"Fabulous!"
"The big tuna."
Mary said: "Are you drunk?"
"I'd better be."
She laughed. "Come on up here."
"What, tonight?"
"Right now."
"Shouldn't," I said. "Should stay in the city. Probably have an early morning. Let's keep it for the weekend."
"Come on up," she said. "Midweek quickie."
"Elegantly put."
"You want elegance or action?"
"See you in an hour."

I hung up. I was sweating, so I removed my suit coat. Michelle appeared. Late twenties, Wharton MBA, five eleven, face of a debutante who's seen Las Vegas, dancing green eyes, white silk blouse, cashmere skirt. "That your woman, beckoning you home?"

I let the inaccuracy of her last word sit. "Maybe."
"Is it true she's a doctor?"
"Sure."
"What kind?"
"Surgeon."
"A woman with sharp knives."

I laughed, took a drink of champagne. Michelle draped herself on me. She smelled of serious perfume and taboo adventure. She took my glass, raised it. "To the hero. The man who brought the bacon home to GTF." She drank off the three swallows that remained, handed the glass back.

"Nothing to it," I said, tasting sweet praise, relishing it, this ego's never-can-get-enough-of-it foie gras.

"In a past life you must have been a warrior," she said.
"I have no idea."
"I'll have to do a regression analysis on you sometime."
"Does that hurt?"
"Not in the right hands." Her arm was around my waist, her

body warm against me. "Meanwhile, I'll bet that under all your whatever, you're also a sweet guy."

"No."

"Are too!"

"Negative. Steel and ripcord to the bone."

Tom Blackwell saw us and headed our way. Michelle laughed, kissed my cheek. "Oh, and this memory thing," she said. "I want to know all about that."

"Nothing to know."

"Tom," said Michelle. "The chief, here. What's his memory trick?"

Tom worked for me. My best writer. Twenty-six, dark hair, dark eyes, black wool turtleneck, dark-gray wool trousers, thin black calfskin belt, black tasseled loafers. "No trick," he said. "The man can simply remember everything ever said in a meeting."

"True?" asked Michelle, looking at me.

"For some reason."

"Yet you can't remember your past lives?"

I shrugged.

Tom produced a bottle of champagne, refilled my glass. He put an arm around Michelle. "Are you tipsy, O'Malley?"

"Close if not there!"

***

An hour later I made it to Grand Central, I'm not sure how, and got a late train to Tarrytown. A raw wind and dropping temperature. Mary's BMW at the curb. I got in the passenger side. She was in gray sweats, running shoes and a ski parka. The car smelled of leather and engine heat. In the green dashboard lights Mary looked to me like treasure on exhibit, glowing.

"Congratulations, advertising man of the year."

"Thanks, and where's my prize?"

"Thought you'd never ask." She leaned over, kissed me, simultaneously unzipping her parka. Under it she was naked. I sought her lips, kissed her hungrily. Substantial breasts pale and pendulous in the car's malachite light. Her weight pushing me back against the car door. I was sixteen again, in my father's 1960 Plymouth parked a mile off the road in Jamestown, New York, with Julianne Calasandro, blood pumping hard to my flushed face and dilated primary arteries. We kissed, fondled. Car windows fogged over. A few minutes later we were speeding up Route 9 on a mission. When we got to Mary's house it was snowing sideways. Mary parked in her driveway and we walked to her porch. I put my arm around her to shield her from the wind.

***

Inside we had brandy, and a shower together, the hot water pelting our skin, warming us. Her hands soaping me slowly. We walked to her bedroom enrobed in fluffy towels. In her bed I mounted up and snort-screamed, part bull, part devil. She was spread beyond physical possibility and, hands to my buttocks, pulling me in, her pelvic bone indurate, a true stone. The sex was what I always asked of it: passion, pleasure, and forgetting. Later someone said unwanted words: "I love you."
Not I.

> *I'm one hundred feet tall, splendid in my double-breasted suit. I tower over Niagara Falls, astride the raging river feeding it, terrified of going over. Three boats pass under my legs, and I recognize them as toys I had when I was a boy. My favorite was an old-fashioned pleasure boat with a long, shallow hull and little seats inside. When I was eight, my aunt Chloe had brought it back from a big toy store in Buffalo. It was of a kind used at the turn of the century on the Niagara River. In my imagination I peopled it with a guide, a steersman and ten passengers, all of whom I named. As the boat bobs past, I grab for it but can't catch it. Over it goes, disappearing into the mist at the bottom of the waterfall. The people! Who'll save the people?*

I awoke, perspiring. Only a dream. Still, dread and loss sat on my chest like birds of prey. I rolled over, in hope of breathing easier, and put my arms around Mary. She awakened, and a fleeting thought of telling her the dream nuzzled my brain, but I chased it, got out of bed and started across her bedroom toward her closet.

And somewhere, near above, the mad rustle of wings. No, just bedcovers being thrown back. She was behind me on the carpet.

"Darling."

I turned. She put her arms around me, pulled me very tight, then stepped back, held me at arms' length. I took in her face, a little puffy yet from sleep: excellent bones, steady brown eyes set at perfect width, high forehead across which the faint lines of early middle age intimated themselves.

"I've been thinking," she said.

"About what?"

"About what you need. Count three before you react. I want you to move in with me."

"That won't work. I have to be in the city."

"You can commute."

"Never."

"Come here," she said, leading me back to the bed. I sat, awkwardly. "Look at me." I did. "I need more than I'm getting from you."

"You're getting all there is."

"Move in. Try it for six months."

I shook my head. "I need space . . . freedom."

"Well I need to think about my future. Are you part of it or not? I want a family. What do you want?"

The future, in anything outside my work, looked to me precisely as it had for years: a movie screen gone dark between the preview and the feature.

"Come on, Jack, talk to me."

I couldn't.

***

The train swung toward New York. Irvington, Dobbs Ferry, Hastings-on-Hudson, Yonkers. At each stop men and women got on, coats buttoned against the cold, settled into seats, opened newspapers. On the right the Hudson was a massive slash across the landscape, a wound beyond healing.

I surveyed it and thought: *The inability to talk, and you an advertising man.* The inability to say: I can't love, but if I could I would love you. Love. The toxic place, a room with incense, day-old marijuana butts, and a floor strewn with broken crockery. *Never again, thank you very much.*

The train pulled into Bronxville. Gordon Fulsome came into my car from the platform with a dozen other people. He wore an overcoat, black dress gloves and a British tweed cap. I waved; he grinned and came down the aisle. There was a seat next to me and he slid in. He smelled of expensive cologne.

Gordon was a tenaciously hardworking man with a limited imagination and a devotion to suburban living. He was also a reformed single who in his youth made any escapades of mine look tame. Something about which he had convenient amnesia.

"Hey, *hey*," he said, clapping my back. "What the hell you doing up here?"

"I came up late, after the party. You'd left."

"Mary?"

"Sure."

"Good. Nobody wants you out tomcatting behind her back, running off like the middle-aged teenager you are, holing up where we can't find you. Now that we're in the chips, you gotta be on call twenty-four hours a day."

"Listen to you."

"In fact, this may be the time for you to get married, settle down."

My fist came down hard on the armrest of my seat. Gordon's head snapped my way. He tried to read my face.

"What?"

"This some kind of fucking conspiracy? Last night Mary wanted me to move in. Had suburbanhood, fatherhood and God knows what all else all planned out for me. Jesus. Marriage. Been there, screwed that up."

"Fine." A moment passed. "I forgot you were married once," said Gordon. "Wasn't it more a hippie experiment in communal living?"

"Pretty much."

"All you flower children in San Francisco."

"That was us."

"And you were what? A folksinger?"

"No."

"Poet, then. Till you smartened up and learned how to make money."

"Bet your ass," I said.

"Traded poetry for Mercedes-Benz. Not a bad deal."

I kept my gaze out the train window. The grime on the outside of the glass obscured the view.

He lowered his voice to conspiracy level. "Thing about this deal is the math. Love the profit that'll come out of forty million. The bucks we're generating for the company — for *us!*"

"Major bucks," I said.

Gordon shifted his weight and I knew what was coming.

"Thing about you, though," he said, "what the hell do you need with more money? How many more ladies can you impress? New suits can you buy? More trips can you take? How much better wine can you drink?"

"The answers, in reverse order, are better, lots more, lots more, and many more."

"Unreal."

"And you," I said. "How many more snow blowers do you need? How many more station cars?"

"Hey, I've got a family. Wife to feed and clothe, kids to insure and educate."

"You can do that already."

He shrugged. I slapped him on the knee, grinned. Truce. The train crossed a bridge over the Harlem River. Manhattan awaited, beckoning, the morning sun glinting off office towers, threatening to blind anyone who looked directly at it. We entered the tunnel at 125th Street, lumbered along in the dark, came into Grand Central. Gordon and I exited the train and followed a throng of commuters.

And from somewhere came the music.

They were along the near wall of the concourse: a dozen people, surrounded by junk. Shopping bags, stained pillows, a filthy blanket, cardboard boxes, remnants of food. The odor of failure, real or imagined. Two people were standing apart. A man and a woman. On his head he wore a gray rag, like a turban. And she — an old cloth coat, woolen hat pulled low, flute to her lips, playing. The man swaying to the music. I slowed a step, for no reason. Gordon hustled me along.

"Fuckin' homeless people," he said. "Oughta clean 'em outa here."

"Don't worry. The place is going to be cleaned up. Renovated."

"The sooner the better," said Gordon. "Relocate the hell out of them."

"To Bronxville?"

"Ha, ha."

"They didn't choose their life," I said.

"Fuck they didn't!"

We walked across the concourse. I suddenly had an odd sense of time. A schism akin to déjà vu. Gordon said something I didn't hear. "Pardon?"

"I said, the thing I love about getting Mercedes, aside from the money . . . ."

"Tell me."

"It puts us up there with the Ogilvies, the J. Walters, the heaviest hitters."

"For sure," I said.

"And about bloody time."

"Bragging rights," I said.

"Big time."

We angled past the information booth, exited the doors on the Forty-second Street side and turned west. The sidewalk was packed.

"Cold," said Gordon. "Feels like December for Christ's sake."

Five steps from Vanderbilt Avenue, I stopped. Gordon continued for a step or two, and turned.

"What's the matter?" he asked.

"What was she playing?"

"Who?"

"That flutist back there."

Gordon shook his head in confusion. We walked a few more steps. I stopped again. "Can't be."

"Can't be what?"

"I think I'm going back."

"Why?"

"I may know her . . . ."

"You joking?"

"I'll see you at the office."

At the station doors a jam of people; then I was back inside, past the newsstand, down the esplanade. The music again. Crisp, staccato notes. I came to the information booth, looked past. She was there, just in from Track 23. Her chin up, face up, flute at a jaunty angle.

I took a step toward her.

Two

"Jack. So you've finally come. You look surprised. It's me, oui Jacques, mon amour, c'est moi."

Above her, above the commuters, the station walls and ceiling shimmered, all part of a mirage. And in the forefront, talking to me, was Emily.

"My," she said, "you've changed, but look who's talking." I had no words, was a gigantic eye, no brain, no conscience, an optic nerve on a stalk of ice.

"Still thin, still good-looking. Oh, nice clothes. I like your watch. Is success wool and skin and Italian leather? Are your ears plastic? Do you like my coat? Thought your little ex-wife was all tucked away somewhere safe and snug? Welcome to America."

My ears were ringing now with something that wasn't music; the dark racing of blood, the white noise of shock.

"Wednesday, October thirtieth, the twenty-first year, fourth month, and third day since our day in the sun — remember?"

She began humming "Here Comes the Bride," swaying. She curtsied, moved past me, imitating a formal processional walk. The hem of her coat down, dragging on the floor. Her smell — unwashed wool, yesterday's urine.

"Emily?" I said.

"Mais oui, chéri, c'est moi."

I had no words, so I grabbed her shoulder. Under the coat she was bony thin. She put a hand over mine. I saw raw red skin, broken nails, obtruding veins. On the back of my hand her fingertips were rough as steel wool. She looked past me, eyes wide. "Who's this?"

It was Gordon, at my side.

We three stood a second, frozen, then Emily turned and ran. She moved fast, through the crowd, out of sight at a track entrance.

***

"Get me out of here," I said.

We left the station, got a cab. Inside, I slumped against the door.

"Jesus Christ," I said.

"That was your wife?"

"Couldn't have been."

"Why the French?"

"She's . . . was from New Orleans. Liked to speak it. Just — you know — for fun."

"So that was her?"

"No, no, can't be. But she knew me."

"And how long has it been since you've seen her?"

"Nineteen years."

***

Gordon and I sat on a six-foot-long leather couch facing Carl Greenberg. Carl was the founder and controlling partner. His office was an enormous L-shaped room with large windows facing east and south. Faux-antique furnishings with a touch of country club. The centerpiece was his huge oval beaten-copper desk, behind which he sat, looking like a character actor overplaying a successful advertising man as pieced together by a Hollywood rewriter. Domed head, aggressive jaw, and round, orange-framed eyeglasses. Small, boyish manicured hands. An ash-tipped, seven-inch Te Amo cigar wedged between the first and second fingers.

"Carl, you gotta hear this," said Gordon. "We just ran into Jack's ex-wife. And guess what? She's a whatdyacallit — bag lady."

"Say again?"

"His wife. Homeless lady in Grand Central. We shit you not."

"Might not be her," I said.

"She either is or she isn't," said Carl.

"Then I have to say she isn't."

"The man's in denial," said Gordon.

"Look!" I said. "Fuck it, alright? If it's her . . . okay, if it's her . . . I'll deal with it. Let's move on. Let's have our damn meeting."

"Wait, wait, wait," said Carl. "You're telling me you just saw your ex-wife who's — what is she?"

"Homeless," said Gordon.

"As in — "

"Street person."

"— a street person," Carl continued, "and you want to go on, business as usual?"

"I said I'd deal with it!"

"Hey," said Carl, "okay." To Gordon: "Why's he so touchy?"

"You run into your ex-wife who's a bag lady," said Gordon, "you wouldn't be touchy?"

"Guys," I said, "do me a favor? Business as usual right now. Can we do that?"

Cigar smoke hung midair. Carl shrugged, removed his phone handset from its desk unit. "Get me Charlie Wend," he said, and hung up. Charlie ran our Chicago office.

"Donovan just called me," said Carl. Donovan was senior VP, marketing, at Mercedes, and our main contact. "They're throwing even more dollars than we thought at us." His phone buzzed, and he picked up. "Charlie, I'm sitting here with Jack and Gordon.

— 14 —

Ready for this? Jack thinks he ran into his ex-wife he hasn't seen since no one knows when and she's a bag lady in Grand Central Station." He listened for a second, cupped the handset.

"He says that's weird shit."

I sat forward, removed my suit coat, threw it aside. "Can we not talk about this?"

Inside, I was weak. Stomach fluttering. Vertigo. Have to hang on. *Her hands. Couldn't be her hands. Hers were artist's hands, sculpted, skilled, perfect.*

Carl was talking to Charlie again: "Listen, Mercedes upped the ante, added extra mayo. Full print run first quarter, all new creative; full TV schedule starting probably as early as January, right on through to sweeps. That not enough? Throw in all collateral and direct mail. Love it? I love it, Jack loves it, Gordon loves it. Get back here like pronto. Fuck Friday, get here tomorrow. Where's Hopkins? L.A.? Get him back too. Screw Chicago — what's the town ever done for us?" He listened, chuckled, hung up.

"Jack, here's where we have to be careful. Remember when we landed the personal card? Got cocky, overconfident, changed strategy midstream, almost blew it. Not this time. Racing, Jack, the megahook, all the work you did on that. We're agreed? Racing, the glamour, glitz, men and machines at the limit and all that shit — that's our anchor."

"Absolutely," I said. "It's what we sold them."

"No one knows this account like you. You've got this client by the balls — they love you, think you're the Hemingway of advertising. So now, who do you want working with you on this? On the copy side."

"Tom Blackwell."

Carl drew on his cigar, exhaled a long pencil of smoke rising forty-five degrees. I watched it rise and rise, then collide with the cloud of haze that hung below the ceiling.

"Tom ready for this?"

"Absolutely. The only possible choice."

"Okay. And if you have to hire more people, hire them. Book your creative group into someplace — Troutbeck, Tarrytown Hilton, Bucks County — someplace out of town, away from the phones. Run some sessions, the brainstorming shit you're a genius at, come back when you've got stuff to show me'll blow the top of my head off."

"Sure," I said. "Hell yes."

"And lunch today — you, me, Gordon, O'Malley, bring Blackwell along if you want."

"Super."

"Eight years, guys, right? Doesn't seem long. We've dreamt about this, the big catch."

"Damn right."

"And now — megabucks. Rope it in, ride this bull to gold."

Three

I walked from Carl's office to mine. I was an actor, doing a role, on a very bad night. I had to cling to the script, no matter what. I passed a nook with a countertop and a coffee machine. Tom Blackwell and Michelle were measuring coffee into a filter with the concentration of conspirators measuring blasting powder for a bomb.

"Chief," said Tom.

"Good morning."

"Where did you go last night?" asked Michelle. "We were looking for you. We did some clubs, figured you'd want to go."

"I was otherwise disposed."

"Oh," said Tom. "The doctor was in."

Michelle assessed me with raised eyebrows.

"What I want to know," I said, "is why all this high-priced talent is standing around a kitchenette making coffee."

"Right," said Michelle. "I was just leaving." She took my arm and walked me along the hallway. "Wished you could have joined us last night."

"What would you have done with me?" I asked.

"Wicked things."

"Next time for sure then."

In my outer office my secretary, Irene, leaned against her desk. Her hair was pulled severely back and her black lipstick made her face a phantasmic white. She held my daily diary, the black polish of her long fingernails jarring against the rich red leather of the diary cover. She wore a long black dress secured tightly at the hips by a wide leather belt sporting a dozen silver studs. She smiled, revealing her bold white teeth. Then she stopped smiling.

"Hangover?"

"No," I said.

"You look a little blue around the gills."

"I've had a shock." I told her what had happened.

Before she could respond, a troop of people arrived: Tom, Michelle, Bill Conway — another of my writers — and Morris Imelweiss, a senior account man. They encircled me.

"We heard," said Tom. "About your wife."

"Is it true?"

"It might have been her."

Michelle pressed on: "So was it her or wasn't it?"

Irene's phone rang. She leaned across her desk to pick it up. "Mr. Transit's office, may I help you." She listened, cupped the mouthpiece. "Mr. Clifton, at ICM."

"I'll take it inside." And I beat a retreat from that mob. Clifton was a client. We talked for twenty minutes about a TV campaign that was about to break. After we finished, I sat back. A sort of flash in my head . My first thought: I'm having a stroke. Then images, like a long-forgotten black-and-white movie.

> I come up the narrow stairs, open the door. Emily stands in our kitchen, hand on her hip. Next to her, two suitcases. What's this? I say. I've packed your things, she answers. Why? I want you out. Why? You know why. All because of a job? It's not just a job, she says. It's selling out. You've sold your fucking soul, and you only get one. You've gone crazy, I say.
>
> Sudden movement. She picks a plate up from the counter and throws it at my head.

My office. I'm fine — I'm in my office! Everything quiet, peaceful, in its place. Fred Astaire was in place. On my wall, to the left of my door, the full tuxedo, cummerbund, and tie, tacked with care for display and amusement. At the cuffs, latex surgeon's gloves ("And you think *I'm* weird," Irene had said when I added those). And above the shirt collar — him, it — my prized Fred Astaire mask. Next to him, the print of my Motherwell nude, paint all in motion, some semblance of a woman's body trapped in the painter's frenzy. My Motherwell nude. To the left, my corner windows, and through them westward to the corner building facing me, and beyond that to the top spindles of St. Patrick's Cathedral. Comforting Gothic spires jutting above flat surfaces of steel and granite. My comforting Gothic spires. Next to the windows, my glassed-in shelf of model racing cars. My red Ferrari Testarossa. My silver Mercedes gullwing. My Jaguar D-type in the blue livery of the Ecosse team, circa 1959. Along the expanse of wall, Veloxes of three ad campaigns: the award-winning vodka campaign, the award-winning credit card campaign, and the award-winning Caribbean tourism campaign. Finally, my two shelves of books. Ogilvy on advertising, *The City in Slang, The Elements of Style, Eros and Language*, my Henry Miller novels, advertising annuals, photography annuals. Everything was in place. Everything ordered, peaceful. *I am Jack Transit. I know exactly who I am.*

A knock at the door.

"Yes," I said.

Irene came in, eyes narrowed inquisitively. In her hand a cup of coffee, steam rising.

"Jack, musta been terrible, this morning. Drink this." She held the cup out to me. The coffee was hot and bitter.

"When's the IDC meeting?"

"Eleven."

"And lunch is . . . ?"

"Twelve-thirty. You don't want to talk about it?" She came close to my desk, peered down at me.

"There's nothing to talk about. Some bag lady, mistook me for someone."

"What did she say?"

I looked at Fred Astaire and thought: Save me.

"So was it her?"

Skin sagging, gray clumps of hair, coat hem dragging.

"'Cause if it was, you can't just sit here like this, pretending it didn't happen."

I took a breath, steeled myself. "Please find out which conference room the IDC meeting's in. Okay?"

She left. My phone rang and I picked up. It was Gordon.

"So you gonna be okay?"

"Fine."

"It's gotta be a shock."

"Not really."

"I've been thinking. My considered advice? Ignore the whole goddamn thing. Just like you have been."

I went silent.

"Listen," he said. "Fulsome's third law: never give the past an inch. Banish its ass. Why? Cause it'll eat your liver. Okay? Look it up."

I laughed at that.

***

Tom knocked at my door. He had a sheaf of papers under his arm.

"I've got copy and concepts for IDC ads. Good time?"

"Sure," I said.

Tom was unusual: a man who, unlike most at his age, had defined himself thoroughly. This was something I liked; it showed in his work and came from a first-class intelligence and an unusual education: a classics degree from Harvard.

We sat at a round glass table near my windows. He handed me five pages. Headlines, line drawings, body copy.

"Drawings just for position. Think photography."

I laid four sheets on my desk, retained the fifth, studied it. Drawing: man on a train, laptop computer on his knees. Headline: COMMUTER COMPUTER.

"Idea for photography," said Tom. "We take stock shots, scan them into the Mac, scan in product, create the shot that way. Here."

He handed me a photograph of a man on a train. "Just scan the laptop right onto his knees."

I studied it, nodded, and picked up the second ad. Drawing: astronaut in a space capsule, deep space visible through a window, laptop on his knees. Headline: WRITE HOME. Tom handed me a NASA photo on which his drawing was based.

The third one: man and woman on a grassy bank, large trees nearby, laptop on man's knees. Headline: COMPUTE WITH NATURE.

"Pun on commune," said Tom.

"I got it."

Tom handed me a photo. A couple on a grassy bank. The trees stopped me. Huge trunks, bark peeling, knife-shaped leaves. I stared at them and at the couple: young, sitting close. I looked at the trees again, wanted to smell them, waited, then got it, the pungent fragrance of eucalyptus, and with it, music.

> Emily and I sitting. Her lush hair down her back, fingers on the flute, wire-rimmed granny glasses, long legs tucked under her. My arm around her. She leans her shoulder into me; the flute is inches from my face. I feel around my neck my shark-tooth and ostrich-bone necklace, on my neck and shoulders my own long hair, on my forehead my beaded headband. The measured, controlled staccato of her playing. And everywhere, the scent of eucalyptus.
>
> Then the sun's going down over Golden Gate Park and we walk hand in hand toward the Japanese Tea Garden.

"Chief?" said Tom.
"What?"
"You okay?"
"Sure. Actually, gotta hit the head. Stay here, I'll be back."
I was out of my office and walking along the corridor. Stopped at a drinking fountain, bent, drank.

> Emily says, Can I hear your poem? No, I say, it's not ready. Please? Later, I say. She takes my arm. Why not now? She tugs at me, we head off the path, across a lawn to Mallard Lake. Three willows in a row, tall and fragile, the middle one leaning toward the water, its long bows bending to the surface as if to see their own reflections. We sit. Come on. I don't want to. Are you so shy about it?

I went to the men's room. At the sink I stared at my face reflected in the mirror. *I look old.* Touched my tie below the knot, wiped my lips.

The red carpeting of the corridor stretched ahead, toward my office.

Eat your liver.

***

Irene said Tom had gotten a call, had to take it, would be back in a few minutes. I sat looking at his ads. Paper under my fingertips.

> Emily says, Come on, please. I take the paper from my pocket, and read.
>
>> The sunny side of the street,
>> the sunny side of the street.
>> The street is sunny, gray, then blue,
>> then the evening invades the avenue.

I stop. No more. Her look of amusement, fascination. A breeze comes up, lifting willow branches, rustling leaves. Emily's face close to mine, her smile engulfing me, her hand on my arm lightly. Please keep going.

> The sidewalks of New York,
> the sidewalks of New York.
> The sidewalks glisten, glow, then fade,
> then are gone like the trumpets in a Liberty Day
> parade.

That's enough. No. It's so . . . derivative. Of what? Something not me. It *is* you, and it's beautiful. It's too soft, there's no edge, it's not what poetry today is. It's what *your* poetry is.

> How soothing fades the evening light,
> how soothing fades the evening light.
> The light fades then whispers then dies,
> while in the blue-gray night sweet death
> intensifies.

Sweet death? That's what I mean, it's just affectation. Her look: *you're impossible.* She points to the last stanza.

> Hurry sundown, see what tomorrow brings.
> Hurry sundown, see what tomorrow brings.
> The trumpets of living, the quiet of dying,
> the marbles of children, the statues of kings.

I'd like to set that to music. How about this: we do a concert, I play, you read. People will love this poem! An irritation in my eye; I rub it. See, I have no confidence. Why not? I read great poetry, it thrills me. I could never . . . . Never what? Come up to that standard.

Four

I sat a long moment, then called Pete Fleming. Pete was my best friend. We'd known each other for twenty-five years. Been copy cubs together at Ogilvy, when he'd met Emily. He'd seen me through the breakup, two years after which I'd seen him through a divorce. For five years after that we'd done New York as singles, done the Hamptons, done the Caribbean. I'd been best man at his second marriage. We played lots of golf and squash together.

Pete's secretary put me through to his voicemail.

"Pete, it's Jack. Give a call. Weird stuff, blast-from-the-past sort of thing, named Emily."

***

At twelve-fifteen we hit the street — myself, Tom, Carl, Gordon, and Michelle. A cold wind was blowing eastward along the side street and I tightened my scarf about my neck.

"Too goddamn cold," said Tom. "Unseasonable and wrong."

"I love the cold," said Michelle.

"What's to love?" asked Tom. "It's unnatural. All it's produced are the Nordic races, famous for violence and Puritanism. No, give me the southern clime, womb of warmth and easy living."

"Clime?" said Michelle.

"Right, as in climate."

"I know what it means, but it's antiquated."

"I bet if you looked it up it wouldn't say `antiquated.'"

"I don't care what it says. Jack, word maven. Clime. Antiquated or no?"

"Mildly antiquated," I said.

"Wait," said Michelle. "There's no `mildly antiquated.' Something's antiquated or it isn't. Jesus, look at that."

Back from the street near an entrance to an underground parking garage, three disheveled men stood near a large, upright, rusted oil drum in which burned a wood fire. The side of the drum was broken through, and red flames licked out of it. Tom stopped and gestured. "Troy has perished, the great city. Only red flame now lives here."

Michelle said, "Oh, right," and made a face.

"See, O'Malley?" Tom said. "Intelligent discourse is lost on you totally."

Michelle cut in front of me to get to Tom, hit him on the upper arm with her fist. Tom put his fists up. They circled one another. Behind them, the barrel emitting bluish smoke, the flames now shooting from its side as from a dragon. Through this orange-and-gray scrim the ghost-men looked at us with stern, uncurious faces.

"Penthesilea, Queen of the Amazons," said Tom. "Warring woman and hater of men."

"And for good reason," said Michelle.

"Hear that, chief? She hates men!"

"Do you hate men?" I asked.

"Au contraire."

"No French!" I said, much more urgently than I intended. "Could we keep this in English, please?"

Ahead of us Carl and Gordon had come to Vanderbilt and were turning south. I caught up with them.

"Where the hell we going?" I asked.

"The Oyster Bar," said Carl. The Oyster Bar is in Grand Central Station.

"No, no," I said, "not there."

"Bullshit," said Carl. "My usual table in the Saloon. Come on."

I let everyone go on ahead, then followed reluctantly into the taxi portico off Vanderbilt Avenue. Bracing myself, I went through one of the glass doors, listened. Only the perpetual station sound, a low hollow white noise echoing in on itself, consuming the tread of footsteps. The metallic interruption of PA-announced train departures. I stood for a second near the broad marble balustrade, relishing the absence of any music.

"Behold." It was Tom, at my elbow. "The bull, Taurus, unequaled in strength, beloved by Zeus." Tom pointed. "And further on, the twins, Gemini, masters of deception."

I looked up. Seventy feet above us, the dim, washed-out gray expanse of ceiling. Sprinkled across it were stars, and traversing the span was a long bar — a sort of celestial vaulting pole, angling away to the southeast corner. Along this bar were huge figures: dim representations of constellations. An immense crab. The Gemini twins, one holding a lyre, one a scythe. An angel with a beard, holding a club. The bull. A few other shapes were at the far end, but I couldn't make them out.

"They're going to clean all this up," said Tom. "Bring it all back to life. And about time."

We went down the stairs, passed Zaro's deli and were opposite the newsstand beyond which the stairs descended to the Saloon. Tom had opened the big wooden door to the Saloon and turned to let me pass, his free hand raised in courtesy and a courtly supplication, when I heard the first note, then another, and another: distant, distinct, inevitable. I stopped.

"What?" Tom said.

The music continued. I couldn't move.

"Chief?"

"Go on without me. I'll be back."

She was there, in the same spot as that morning, playing Vivaldi this time. She saw me coming from fifteen feet away, stopped mid-phrase, lowered the flute, turned, started off. I kept distance between us, followed her out of the concourse, up toward the waiting room on the Forty-second Street side, to a bench against the back wall. She sat, reached under the bench, brought out her flute case. I knew it well. The black leather over the hard shell was worn now, scarred, but there on top was the bronze plate, inscribed: EMILY LEMOINE TRANSIT.

I stared at those names, equally familiar and alien, three attached train cars returned from how long, in what hell?

She unsnapped the case's clasps, opened it. The red velvet bed (faded now), the extra mouthpiece. She disassembled her flute and laid it down, as years before I'd seen her do daily, putting her baby to bed. Snapped the case shut. Her hands. Claws of a hungry bird. She saw me looking.

"What life can do," she said.

She patted the bench next to her. The gesture chilled me because standing above her, looking down, I was just removed enough to tolerate this scene, but sitting next to her would — horrible! — net me right into it.

I spoke without moving: "What's happened to you?"

"Not a what, chéri, a him."

"Who?"

"Don't you be crafty, now."

I tried to speak calmly. "Where do you live?"

"Palm Springs. Only in New York for the social season."

"Where do you sleep?"

"The Hyatt, the Plaza, the Pierre. Actually, I'm between engagements, got a gig in Taos, end of the month. Crawling there on my belly."

This was an even deeper assault. Not just her awful clothes and rank body. Her mind was broken too. Money could not fix this, nor better food, nor a month of baths.

"So I'm fine, and when I'm not, it's nothing he can't fix."

"Who?"

"Him! The one that sent you."

"No one sent me."

"Ha! Don't you lie — I know he did."

"Who?"

"Him, him, him — with the wings and the body and the undercarriage, hung like dynamite, potent as hot rods. You're his messenger. Oh, as long as we're discussing family, know I'm not in any mood to talk about *her*. Let that be understood. What you're to do is tell me about *him*. They have nothing to do with each other, nor ever will. He lives above us, resides in the eternal, and she is here, partaking of mortality, steeped in it."

The walls were closing in. Nothing existed outside the few square feet of stale station air that contained us.

"Emily, I don't know who you mean."

"I mean you, in another form. You and me, in another form."

Again, silence. To block what I was seeing of her mind, I found myself trying to sense her physically beneath her clothes, as I had when I'd touched her shoulder earlier. Emily had been full-bodied, substantial. She was now wasted, beyond thin.

"How do you eat?" I asked, stupidly.

She spat her reply out: "This is the census? What else, then? What insurance I own? How many cars I have? Shows I attend, charities, political convictions, criminal convictions, trips? Tips? Tits? Two. I have two tits, as you well know, but I prefer the more genteel term: breasts. Of course, they're irrelevant appendages now: I neither attract men nor mother infants. Babies are best impaled and roasted."

She smiled, changed expression. Intimate, conspiratorial. "But tell me about *him*. He's coming?"

I fought to stay focused. "Who?"

"Pegasus! Don't be like that. You always were a touch coy, odd for a man. In Louisiana, men are ramrod straight — not to impugn your masculinity: you had lots of that, for a Yankee." Her high, tinkling, musical laugh sounded more like the Emily I remembered. She touched my forearm.

"He's my father, he misses me, and I want to know about him, so don't you play Frisbee with my brain. Look at me, at *me*. You always were self-centered. Have you grown, seen life, gotten sharper, developed some courage? Know how to stay? Stand? Or only run away again?"

"I never ran away from you."

"Ran, run, from Middle English *ronnen*, to move at a fast gallop." During this a line of spittle had formed at the corner of her mouth, then lengthened to her chin. And I made a decision.

"Emily, will you do something for me?"

She cocked her head. I reached to my back pocket. "If I give you money, will you . . . is there a place for you to go? Get cleaned up, get food?"

I took out my wallet, opened it. Inside, two one-hundred-dollar bills, two twenties, some ones. I extracted them all.

"Okay? Please take this for now." I held the bills to her.

She took them, and defiantly cried out, "Ha! Lucre! Currency of the system! Lifeblood of mediocrity!" She threw the bills into the air. I was stunned by this, stepped back from her. The bills fluttered down between us. "And now, Jack — look, *you* do something for *me*. You ask me about *her*. Now."

A hundred-dollar bill lay on my shoe, and a twenty was between her feet. I knelt to retrieve them.

"Get up!" she barked. "No bowing, no scraping. It's time you knew."

I stood, the money in my hand.

"Minerva is her name," said Emily. "Are you listening?"

I wasn't.

"Christ!" I said. "Why won't you let me help you?"

"She's your daughter."

"Who?"

"Minerva. Forget money. Forget everything you know. You know nothing. Minerva, spelled `M-i-n-e-r-v-a.´ Your daughter, offspring of your loins."

Her face close to mine. The smell intense, gagging. Broken veins in her cheeks, grime in the creases in her neck.

"Entends-tu maintenant? We have a daughter, you and me. You left me July first, nineteen seventy-two, we lived on MacDougal

Street, three rooms, tub in the kitchen, we made love the last time on May twenty-sixth, your birthday. Incense, black lights, I smoked Colombia Gold, you drank Scotch, and we listened to `Abbey Road.´ I came twice, great dark spirals, spinners, wheelagigs, concentric disks. You came once, huge searing liquid gobs of lava burning down into me. Cells split, divided, grew. Result: Minerva LeMoine — don't look for your name on her — you won't find it. Born February twenty-first, nineteen seventy-three, turns guess what next year? Twenty. My age when we met."

White noise in my ears. *Smell of incense, marijuana.* "Stop that."

"C'est la vérité."

I yelled: "You're lying!"

She shrank as if struck, then grinned, a horrid, starving, insane rictus. "Think I'm lying, think I'm crazy, see for yourself, then, got the balls for it? Come meet your daughter, you'll like her, she looks like you, walks like you, smells like you, thinks like you, breathes like you. She comes here, will come out here, will talk to you if I tell her to. Today, when the little hand's on the four and the big hand's on the twelve."

She backpedaled, knelt, picked another bill from the floor — the second hundred — handed it toward me.

"Here." She stuffed the bill into the breast pocket of my overcoat. "For you, Daddy."

***

At the table in the Saloon I raised the glass and, hand shaking, drank off two fingers of scotch. Then two more.

"Bring him another one," Carl said to a waiter.

"So now you know it's her," said Tom.

"It's her."

"What did she say?" asked Michelle.

"Bunch of nonsense — she's obviously sick. Needs all kinds of help." The waiter brought a second drink. "She's irrational. Has some facts right, about dates . . . when we were . . . ."

"What are you going to do?" asked Carl.
"Don't know. She said . . . implied . . ."
"Said what?"
"Nothing."
"We've got to get her off the street," said Tom. "Get her some help."
"I tried to give her money. She threw it back at me."
"Can't we call someone? Police, ambulance, hospital?"
"Not yet," I said.
"Why not?"
"I'm supposed to meet up with her again — at four today."
"Yeah?" said Carl.
"To, uh, to . . . she might show me . . . something."
"Show you what?"
I couldn't say it. Suddenly I stood. "I've gotta get out of here. Need air." And I left them all sitting there.

Five

*O*n Forty-fourth Street the sun was blocked by buildings and the sidewalks were in shade. The air was damp, cold. Hands in my pockets, I walked, not sure where. At Madison turned uptown to Forty-seventh. Frank's was just in to the left. I considered going there but disliked the risk of running into people I knew. Kept walking, and at Forty-eighth turned right. I'd find an anonymous bar on Third Avenue.

In ten minutes I walked into a dark, fake-wood saloon — somewhat downscale, perfect place for me. I doubted anyone I knew would be there. I could think. Tables in the back, not crowded, empty stools at the bar. I took one. Big bartender with handlebar mustache and a scar across his lower lip. I ordered a scotch. The bartender placed it delicately on a paper napkin in front of me. I drank half of it, put the glass down. A nice buzz announcing itself in my head.

Turns guess what next year? Twenty. Can't be. No such thing as my child. *She comes here . . . Today, when the little hand's on the four, big hand's on the twelve. Minerva. Offspring of your loins.*

I raised the glass, put it down. Looked around the bar, caught the bartender's eye.

"Payphone?" I said.

"Downstairs." He pointed.

I slid off the stool, went down the stairs. An alcove with two phones. I put money in one, dialed Mary's office, got her answering machine saying she was unavailable and giving a number to call in an emergency. Hung up, called Pete Fleming again. His secretary said he was out to lunch. Yes, he'd gotten my message. I said I'd call again.

Back at the bar things had picked up. All stools were now occupied but mine. To my right a rail-thin woman talking to a man next to her. He wore a leather coat with a fur collar. On my left a man in a sportscoat that was too large for him. Long hair in a ponytail, diamond ear stud, extremely small wire-rimmed glasses. His right hand wrapped around a beer bottle. On the back of his hand a tattoo: a horseshoe, around the top of which were the words *Good luck*. Around the bottom, *Asshole*.

He saw me looking at it and grinned lopsidedly. "We all get to be stupid once," he said in a broad southern accent.

"What do you mean?"

He held up his hand. "You noticed this." I looked at the tattoo again. "Long story," he said.

I was in no mood to talk.

We drank. "Ah hell," he said. "I've got a little time."

I exhaled, looked away. It didn't stop him.

"I was in Chicago in eighty-two. I was seventeen, chasing a skirt — girl from my hometown. Ex-girlfriend, I'd heard she was up in Chicago, I called her, insisted on going to see her. My buddies back home — Memphis — said it was stupid to go after her 'cause she was like a slut, had slept with half the guys in Memphis one time or another, by now had probably slept with half the guys in Chicago. What was I going after her for? Fact is, I was in love with her, had been since I was about ten. Didn't matter to me what she'd done. I loved her. So I lit out, sayin' I'd find her, marry her, bring her back. Last word from my buddies when I took off was `Good luck, asshole.´"

He drank his beer and I half listened.

"I was what you might call disappointed when I found her. My heart was broke. I mean broke good. Told her goodbye, got real drunk, woke up on a bench looking at Lake Michigan the next morning. This was on my hand. I remembered going for a tattoo sometime the night before, but I thought I was going to get her name put on. Musta changed my mind an' ordered this."

The bartender came by.

"Want another drink?" the man asked. Before I could answer he'd ordered himself one.

I was stuck now. Had to say something. "What about her broke your heart so bad?"

He eyed me enigmatically. "She was pregnant."

"That'll do it," I said.

"'Bout eight months gone. Weird thing . . . she kept saying it was mine — I was the father. That it was like fate that I had called her and everything — come to see her — 'cause she'd never told me, figured I'd have rejected her. So like now I was supposed to be happy about it, this was the happiest day in both our lives. But to me it was just a damn lie because I hadn't even seen her in a year. I told her I loved her but this ruined it. Everything the guys back home said burst into my head. I hit the roof, got out of there fast."

He sipped his beer. I drank my scotch.

"I caught an early bus, and refigured with a calendar. Sure enough, it hadn't been a year since I'd seen her. I'd spent a night with her back home exactly eight months before. At the first stop I turned around and went right back. Burst into her place, woke her up, took her in my arms. We got married a month later, moved up to New Jersey. My son's now nine." He looked at his watch. "Hey, shit, three-thirty. I'm running late."

"What's your name?" I asked.

"Boyd Ratcliffe."

"Jack." We shook hands.

"Your story fascinates the hell out of me," I said. "Want to know why?"

"Sure."

I drank scotch. The buzz in my head a little stronger. "I'm about to meet someone . . . ."

"Yeah?"

"She's — well, she may be my daughter."

"And you're about to meet her?"

"Right. For the first time."

"How old?"

"Twenty. Her mother and I divorced, I didn't know she was pregnant. Now she says I have a daughter."

"Well son of a bitch."

"Yeah. Any advice?"

He put money on the bar, stood. He took a pair of gloves from his sportscoat pocket. "I will say one thing," he said.

"Shoot."

"Fate is all there is — trust it. That and — " He took his right hand in his left so his left thumb was across his right palm. He held his hands up, the back of his right one, with the tattoo, toward me. The index finger of his left hand covered the bottom half of the tattoo, leaving the top of the horseshoe visible, with the two words above it for me to read.

***

Twenty minutes later I put down a tip and left the bar. The temperature had dropped further. I walked west, south, into the Lexington Avenue side of the station. The long walk to the concourse. No music. Emily was at her spot.

Next to her was someone new.

A tall, lean figure with close-cropped auburn hair. A woman, or a girl; right on the cusp. Clearly not dressed as a street person: black skirt, high-heeled, calf-high black boots. Short, tight-fitting black wool jacket over a maroon shirt open at the neck. Some sort of choker necklace. Taller than Emily, her legs long, shapely.

Short hair set off her profile: strong chin, high cheekbones, prominent, straight nose.

I went to them quickly, so my nerve would not have time to fail. Emily saw me coming, faced me. As did the young woman. Large, wide-set gray eyes; in them a depth of something I wasn't prepared for. Her mouth was not what I expected.

Emily put a hand on my arm. "Minerva LeMoine, meet Jack Alan Transit."

Minerva's eyes absolutely blazed into mine. She shifted posture, and I was aware of a great physical urgency, aggressiveness, danger even. She spoke to Emily.

"I said I didn't want to, goddamn it!"

"He's your father, and he wants to meet you."

"He's *not* my father." She bolted, something wild cutting a tether, running for freedom. I said to Emily: "Stay here," and went after Minerva.

She was on an escalator going up to the MetLife Building, and I took the one alongside it. We got to the top more or less together, but she didn't see me — she was looking over her right shoulder, back toward Emily. She walked briskly toward the revolving doors ahead. I followed a few paces behind her, let her go through the doors, followed her.

She moved with grace and strength along the corridor: a young athlete or ballerina. She didn't know I was behind her, and that was fine. I didn't want a footrace so I slowed, hoping she wouldn't turn to look again. The corridor widened out into a lobby at the far end of which were more revolving doors. When she was eight or ten strides from these, I came up behind her.

"Minerva!"

She turned and her hands came up like a boxer's. A sound from her like a growl. Again her mouth surprised me. Wide, full, unlike mine, much more like her mother's. Shot through the gray of her eyes were flecks of iridescent green. They struck me as pinpoints of rage. Very low in her throat she said, "What do you want?"

"To talk to you."

"No!

"Why not?"

Her brow was young and clear, had that aching purity of youth, as if life had not yet intruded on perfect flesh and bone. This brow did a slow contraction, and anger flushed it dark. She dropped her hands and stepped closer. A scent of physical effort came off her.

"The last thing I need is you in my life. When Emily said you'd come, I almost threw up. Get away from me and stay away."

She blurred in front of me: my eyes couldn't hold back how lacerated I was. Strangely, I felt myself small, shorter now than she was, actually looking up at her.

"Now nod once," she said, "so I know you hear me and understand exactly how I feel."

Fate is all there is. Well, maybe it needs some help. Her imperiousness made me angry. Nod, my ass! I measured my words: "First of all, who the hell do you think you're threatening? Second, you want to walk away from me, walk. I don't stop anyone from going anywhere."

"Listen! Think I need a father? It's the *last* thing I need."

A filament of intuition broke through, and I sensed, as a form in the dark, the root of her anger. Or maybe I only guessed. But it softened me. I spoke calmly. "Forget need. Neither of us needs the other. But I'll bet you're confused about me. Do you think I've known about you up till now? Because I never knew you were born. I didn't even know you were conceived. God's truth. I learned about you for the first time this morning."

She gave me a poker face, which was fine. In my business, I study them across conference tables all the time. Hers was amateur stuff: under it I saw a whole layer of pride, which broke into a layer of fear, and beneath that, clear as a readout, my answer.

"You thought I knew. No wonder you hate me."

I wasn't sure enough to reach for her, so I didn't move. I felt I was on the verge of offering a taming hand to a wild animal. She was in limbo, undecided, waiting.

I surprised myself with this next: "Back that way, this side of the newsstand, there's a coffee shop," I said. "Please come on with me, have something to eat, or coffee, or whatever. We owe it to ourselves to know each other a little."

Six

I turned to lead the way back toward the escalator. After a couple of steps, I looked back. Minerva was running at full stride away from me. I shouted after her and pursued her. At the far north side of the lobby she pushed through swinging glass doors and was out and running across Forty-fifth Street and, with just a few strides, all the way under an arch of Helmsley Walk. Her speed bordered on the inhumanly quick. By the time I got to the curb, a truck was crawling past, barely moving. I had to run around its tail, and when I got across she had disappeared.

I ran through the arch. Park Avenue stretched north, and pedestrians were thick, coming toward me, commuters again, returning to the station. But no Minerva. I walked a few steps west on Forty-sixth, cursed, and went back into the lobby of 230 Park. She was not there.

Again inside the MetLife Building, I walked slowly, feeling foolish and suddenly old. Had I been defeated? I went back down the escalator to the station. As this morning, people moved intently in every direction, in a crisscrossing pattern whose only logic was randomness. But no one was stationary, no one stood still amidst it all: no Emily occupied the chosen spot.

I went to it. *This is where she stands and plays.* People rushed by me to trains. I felt an odd, solitary sensation, intensely alone while surrounded by people. After a moment I looked upward. Directly above, high on that gray ceiling, a dim figure. I squinted to make it out. The last of the constellations — feathery, indistinct, cartoonish. White, lacy wings spread back, huge head strained forward, a horse in full flight: Pegasus.

I continued standing, in a strange eddy of time in which everything swirled around me, but where I stood there was no time, no movement. I knew, with solid conviction, that I was waiting for someone.

He emerged from the far right-hand archway at a brisk pace, the soiled white towel wrapped around his head, a simulated turban. The man who'd been with Emily that morning. He passed the information booth, continued toward the waiting room. I moved at an angle to intercept him.

"Hello. Nice to see you again," I said.

He stopped. A small, boyish face, close-set eyes, clean-shaven cheeks, lips slightly cracked and dry. He wore a lightweight khaki jacket and, on his hands, large white gardening gloves.

"You a cop?"

"No, no, I'm Jack, Emily's friend."

He smiled, and I saw that the only teeth he had were the two in front, and they came to neat little points, as if filed.

"That's a relief, 'cause I got business with the cops I don't really need."

He started off again, and I walked along beside him, under the big clock past the phone booths.

"What's your name?" I asked.

"Marvin, but that's not for everyone to know. Basically, I got stuff I oughta be dealing with. I gotta see my lawyer."

"Why's that?"

"They accused me of throwing a beer can on the tracks."

We went into the waiting room, and he slowed.

"How could they accuse me of that? Said it blew out the third rail, caused a collision, and killed about a hundred and fifty people in suits. I said that was impossible. I couldn't have thrown any can, killed any people."

He edged toward a bench; I stayed with him.

"This is what they have to understand. My lawyer will explain it, take the city to court — I've got the time. I couldn't have done it. Know why?"

"No."

"I have an airtight alibi. Guess what it is. Go ahead, guess."

"I can't."

He flung his arms wide. "I drink wine! Is that ironical? A can on the tracks, a third rail blowing out, big explosion, beer on the ceiling, passengers frying by the score, french frying in Budweiser, and all I touch is wine? It's an issue the mayor will be forced to deal with, and then'll be referred to the Supreme Court."

On the bench near us were a well-dressed young man, a middle-aged man with half a dozen shopping bags, and an old woman, who appeared to be asleep. She wore a sweatshirt that said:

New York Giants
Super Bowl Champs 1987

The man in the turban spoke again. "You a friend of Emily's?"

"Yes."

"Nice lady," he said. "Interesting past, complex disposition, bad complexion, dubious future. Who among us — "

"Yaka, yaka, yaka."

This had come from the lady in the sweatshirt. She was peering at us.

"Talk, talk, talk — right, Marvin? Just run it and run it."

Marvin's face reddened. He took me gently by the arm and led me a few paces away. The woman laughed gleefully.

He whispered, "She's unfortunately totally wacko, and the more people who know it the better. For her own good."

"Listen," I said. "About Emily. Where can I find her?"

"You can't."

"Why not?"

"She's gone, just left."

"Left for where?"

"She's traveling."

"But she was just here."

"That was then. Ask anyone, ask this gentleman."

The well-dressed man eyed us.

Marvin said to him: "This gentleman is looking for Emily and I'm explaining that she chose today to begin a journey. One that will take her afield. Am I correct?"

The well-dressed man nodded. The old woman inched closer.

"Mrs. Jenkins," Marvin said to her, "we were discussing Emily, and her travel plans."

She looked me up and down. "Bad season for it. Bad day for it. Best stay home."

"Listen," I said to Marvin, "I want to find Emily. Can you help?"

"That would cost you."

"Cost me what?"

"Whatever you value most."

I had no answer to that. Marvin grinned. "Just as I thought: You don't know what you value most. And they call *me* confused."

"Cut that. Just tell me."

"I'd charge a flat project rate."

"Keep going."

"Basically, I take you to see someone. *The* one. The one who knows. Lady of the mist, lives at the center of the earth, mist rising around her, has powers to see and heal. Listen and guide and make clear; listen and speak and clarify."

I said: "This is a con, isn't it?"

"No, no. Value for money. She's your ticket. She can solve your problem."

"Why don't you just tell me where Emily is?"

"Doesn't work that way. It takes the oracle. And I ain't her."

"Forget it," I said. I left without looking back.

***

I got a cab in the Vanderbilt portico. The driver was a kid with a turned-around Knicks cap. I gave him my address and collapsed back into the seat. I was drained. We headed west, but after a block I changed my mind and told him Eighty-sixth and Lexington. So we headed up Sixth toward the park.

After a moment, the kid said to me: "Cold as shit, huh?"

"Yeah."

"October in the Apple, man, feels like January."

"It does."

"Like get out the coat, the gloves, the scarf, man. Ready for tomorrow?"

"What's that?"

"Fright night, man, Halloween night, Gotham goes bat shit, all right? Like lock your doors, man, look out for Casper the ghost and a flock of vampires."

We entered the park, took the drive north. The wind bent the trees over. We passed a horse carriage in which a couple sat bundled under a blanket. The driver was a young woman in a bright-red coat and a tall black top hat, the summit of which now carried a dusting of snow. As we passed I looked back, to see the couple better. They were kissing and their faces were hidden from view. Again the images. The old movie.

> Emily's face glows pale and lovely in the café's candlelight. She raises a glass.
>
> Happy birthday. Thanks. I have a special treat. Yes? He'll be here anytime.
>
> Who? And she names a famous poet, one of my idols, the only living one.
>
> He'll be here? Is here. She stands. I follow her gaze. There he is, coming toward us, slim and dapper, the sweeping white hair, the famous long face, narrow eyes, dominant nose. I stand, Emily does introductions, we sit, she grinning at me, he smiling tightly, myself in an agony of self-consciousness.

I learn that his agent and Emily's are friends. Emily has gone to great length to arrange this, and the poet is ours for the evening. Wine, bread, pasta, espresso, brandy. Then back to our apartment where he sits primly on our couch, smoking a French cigarette, much as in his pictures. I take his book from my shelf. He reads one, two, three poems, closes the book, his finger still in the place, and says: And now your turn.

No, I can't. Emily: Come on. It wouldn't be right. He: Please? You don't understand, I'm . . . none of mine . . . my poems —

Emily's hand on my arm, and myself caught between two wishes, to read and to run. I take a sheaf of papers from a drawer. Here's one I've been working on.

> Your smile
> is my
> horn of plenty.
> In its humid center
> grows a tangle
> of aberrant flowers.
> When they wilt
> a sulfur wind roars,
> skulls skid across cartops,
> graves grow in faces.
> When they bloom
> incense glows red wisdom,
> words dance with hoofer-ghosts
> and the city is
> mangoes, diamonds and basswood tea.

His face upturned, chin jutting, eyebrows raised, eyes on mine. I'm not sure you need `humid.´ As for `basswood,´ yes, it is synonymous with linden, from the leaves of which tea is made. I just don't know if anyone calls it basswood tea, but I applaud using the lesser-known name, for freshness. Every other word is right.

Bravo. But are you an incipient romantic? Great danger lies that way. Don't answer. Please, read me more poems.

"Mister? We're here."

I paid the fare and got out.

"Gotham on Halloween night, man," said the driver. "Like get epic, all right?"

I had no idea what he meant.

I crossed the street and entered the Uptown Squash Club, changed into shorts, T-shirt, sweat socks and running shoes. "Memory," I said aloud. "Christ, I hate it!" I headed for the treadmill. I set it at my usual seven miles per hour and began to run, but after only a minute and a half I had no air, so I slowed the machine and stepped off. My breathing was shallow and my calves were stiff. Men were running on treadmills on either side of me. I waited a moment, listening to the rhythm of their running, the slap-slap-slap of running shoes. I set my machine at six point five and resumed. I ran, and ran, and ran.

Later, I lay in the sauna, the heat around me like a blanket. When I ran, time had ceased to exist, and I could feel it wanting to come back now, to plague me, and I fought to keep it away, along with memory and conscience. I want only this body, this sweat, this heat. No mind, no needs, no past, no future.

I showered, dressed, and took a cab to West Seventy-sixth Street. I have a one-bedroom apartment on the fifth floor of a building off Central Park West. I went into my bedroom. My large four-poster Shaker bed. I was glad I had made it that morning; finding it unmade would have depressed me. I got out of my suit and into worn corduroy trousers, a long-sleeved cotton shirt, and leather slippers.

Back in my living room I examined the paintings and prints on my wall as if they were someone else's: my nineteenth-century Spanish watercolor, my three Japanese prints, and my large abstract oil painting by a New Jersey artist who was the cousin of a proofreader at my agency. The painting, dominated by thin, crisscrossing red and blue lines, looked like a road map of a lightly populated rural county, and was called *Major Meat I*. Tonight it made me anxious.

Suddenly my mind was racing, on a search-and-destroy, but what it was after I didn't know. Seeking escape, I snared my TV remote from the coffee table, sat, and clicked on the news. The familiar face of Tom Brokaw soothed me for a few moments, warmed me to the first few layers of my epidermis, and I waited for the warmth to go deeper, penetrate somewhere beneath the skin, but that didn't happen.

I got up again, crossed the room to my bar, poured two fingers of scotch into a squat cocktail glass, and carried it back to my couch. I took one aromatic, jolting sip, clicked off the TV, sank deeper into the couch, and decided there was nothing to do but think.

Somewhere above me, circling, waiting, the birds again: the raven of thought, the hawk of emotion. The realization came, when it did, as one of their brethren — a mosquito on a humid night, a falcon on a hunt: my apartment, my carefully furnished nest, my oasis in the city, a place where I could always find refuge and comfort, suffered from an obvious, horrible condition: it was profoundly, unacceptably, threateningly empty.

Later I stood at my windows and looked up to see a huge moon looming above a building to the south. The moon lacked a tiny piece at the bottom to make it full. Its color was pale and repellent. A mammoth detached eyeball seen from the back.

I walked to the phone. After three rings Mary answered.
"Hi, it's me."
The slightest pause. "Oh?"
"You surprised?"

"What time is it?"

"Elevenish. How was your day?"

"Long . . . six surgeries."

"Tell me about them."

Enough of a hesitation to tell me I was in trouble. "Why are you calling?"

"Can I tell you about my day? What's happened to me?"

Her voice came back angry: "You're taking a lot for granted."

"I know that."

"Let's not pretend this morning didn't happen, okay?"

"No. But something happened afterward. Listen." I launched into the narrative, took her straight through it.

"Well, Jesus," she said when I finished.

"Yeah."

"What are you going to do?"

"I don't know. I'm stuck. What would you do?"

"Try to help her I guess."

"Help her what?"

"Get off the street; somewhere safe."

"If I did, would you help me?"

"How?"

"Provide backup . . . something."

There was a pause and I could feel her thinking. "No."

I let it sit, and she went on. Her voice low, intimate. "I'm not the one."

My naïveté compelled me on: "Why not?"

"Not after this morning. I've stopped kidding myself. I'm thirty-six and alone. And guess what? I don't plan on being alone when I'm thirty-eight or forty."

"I can't blame you."

"I play healer all day long and it's not something I can come home to. Not a role — sure, a role I've played with other men, now that I think of it, but not a role for me now. I have to find a man who's *been* healed, and is ready to . . . ." She stopped.

"Ready to love."

— 47 —

"For my own self-interest. My own life."

We both seemed to disappear; for a moment I thought we'd been cut off, so quiet was the line. Then: "I just don't know what more to say to you, Jack."

Just me and the moon and the TV remote and the silence of my room. "Say I can see you just once more — not now, but later sometime." Silence. "I'll pick a time when . . ."

"When what?"

But `when´ wasn't the operative word. "If," I corrected, "if I have something to offer you."

Her voice changed, got broken and breathy, and I knew that what she said cost her: "You son of a bitch, I could so easily love you."

She hung up.

Later I fell asleep to an orchestral concert on A&E featuring a female harpist playing something ancient I didn't recognize.

There I was again, a giant, standing above Niagara Falls, the river raging between my legs, powering toward the falls' lip. In the river now were enormous ice floes the size of houses, and they crashed along, colliding with one another, careening toward the falls. My excursion boat was tiny among them, bobbing in the black water, and I reached for it but couldn't get it, and the current pulled it away. I was naked. I hated the nakedness, hated standing in a wide stance above the water, exposed. The spray from the river flew up, was freezing against my legs, abdomen, and scrotum. My penis shrank in the cold. I tried to move but could not, and I saw why: large stakes were driven into the soft riverbank and each of my ankles was tied with hemp rope to a stake.

From above me came a cry. Circling at a height of twenty feet was a huge bird. Not a bird but, rather, a flying creature I could not identify. It had wide,

feathered wings and leathery skin, a small head and an enormous beak such as flying dinosaurs had.
It saw me and prepared to dive.

I awakened terrified, and sat on the edge of the bed. My shirt was wet with perspiration, as was the sheet where I'd lain. Three A.M. Went to the refrigerator for a beer. Stood at my window. The moon was gone from view and freakish lights made a backdrop somewhere beyond the park. Cold night, cold streets.

My shirt open to my chest, my silver necklace and peace pendant dangling, my hair gathered in a ponytail. Emily next to me, cotton granny dress with paisley print, headband of flowers. Flowing behind her, the veil: antique white lace veil, once her mother's and grandmother's.

Musicians, friends, strangers follow, and we walk in procession out of Golden Gate Park and into the Haight. Stop at an intersection to dance. Banners flying, people leaning out of second-story windows, shouting, laughing. Someone hands Emily a flute, and she plays "When you come to San Francisco." We dance up Ashbury past Waller and Frederick. I take Emily's hand, turn her; we stand in the street, embracing.

We did it, I say. So call me Mrs. Transit. Mrs. Transit. Love me forever? she asks. Oh, yes.

Seven

As I left my building the next morning the doorman handed me my morning *Times*.

"Thanks."

"Hasn't gotten any warmer," he said.

I walked to Central Park West. The wind raked up the avenue, carrying grit, newspapers, trashbags. I got a cab to the office.

Irene greeted me at the door of my suite.

"Pete Fleming just called. He's at his office. IDC meeting at ten, Mercedes at eleven. Coffee?"

"No," I said. "And listen. Yesterday. I know you were trying to help."

She ran a tongue over heavy lipstick.

"Want me to stop trying?"

"No, no. I need all the help I can get. I'll be with Tom Blackwell."

Tom's door was open and I looked in. He sat at his desk staring at the screen of a Mac SE; on his head was a set of Sony Walkman headphones. He saw me and removed the headphones.

"Morning, chief."

"Morning." I went in and sat on a chair facing him. Behind him was a credenza on which sat a classical bust, Plato presumably. Tom placed the headphones on it.

"How are things in antiquity?" I asked.

"Where?"

"Mythology, the classics. You did study the classics."

"Misspent youth. Poring over Thucydides while intelligent people went to business school."

"Pegasus," I said. "What's his story?"

"Flying horse." He eased his chair back, laced his fingers behind his head. "Let's see. Was tamed by Bellerophon, of whose sad end Homer sings, Book Six of the *Iliad*. Latin writers loved him too. Pindar gets him best: `A winged steed, unwearying of flight, sweeping through air swift as wind shear.´ Wind shear is actually my improvement. Literally, it's `swift as a gale of wind,´ which doesn't scan."

"Where'd he come from?"

"Sprang from the Gorgon's blood when Perseus killed her."

"What'd he do?"

"Magic. Wherever his hoof touched, up jumped a pure spring. Poets loved that because he performed this trick most often on Helicon, mountain of the Muses. Lesson: Always work your wonders where the Muses abide. Guarantee you immortal fame in verse. Anyway, Bellerophon — no, he's not a famous Spanish golf professional — Greek youth, all the requisite beauty of face and form: Bellerophon suffered a hopeless longing for Pegasus. He got hold of — stop me if I get long-winded. Is this what you wanted to know?"

"No idea. Keep going."

"He got hold of a magic bridle made of gold . . . where the hell'd he get that? Ah! Came to him in a dream — don't you love it? When he awoke, there it was beside him. Slipped it on Pegasus. Took a page out of Minerva's book there, come to think of it."

I came forward in my chair. "Come again."

"Just cross-referencing. Old habit."

"You said Minerva. What about her?"

"She invented the bridle; first mortal ever to tame a horse."

"What else about her?"

"Minerva? Jumping around here. Let's see. Jupiter was her father."

"Who was her mother?"

"Didn't have one, which made her furious. Juno was Jupiter's wife, but she had no part in it. Minerva sprang full-born from Jupiter's forehead. Hell of a warrior: `gray-eyed battle goddess,´ Homer calls her. I'm mixing Greek and Roman sources here — sorry. Anyway, she — Minerva — was very accomplished: goddess of the city, the defender of civilized life. I forget what else she did."

"Pegasus — did he ever send messengers?"

"To whom?"

"Anyone. Lost souls . . . I don't know."

"Don't think so."

"He have anything to do with music? Flutes . . . anything?"

"Not that I remember."

I got up, and Tom said: "So what's the story? Why do you need to know all this?"

"I doubt very much that I do."

He nodded skeptically, and I left.

Back in my office I called Pete Fleming, and this time got him. I asked him to have lunch with me, but he had a business lunch. I said I had to see him, and we arranged that I'd come over to his office at noon.

At ten of twelve I ducked out of my meeting and five minutes later was in a cab heading downtown on Fifth Avenue. I entered the huge high-ceilinged lobby of a refurbished nineteenth-century stone building, with an elevator the size of a studio apartment. I rode up alone and pushed through the doors marked FLEMING & MYERS. At the far side of a dramatic, spare reception area, behind a nine-foot-long aluminum desk, sat a receptionist. She was disconcertingly young. I went up to her.

"Hi. Jack Transit for Pete Fleming."

"Is he expecting you?"

"Yes."

She buzzed me through another set of doors. I took the wide, carpeted corridor toward Pete's office. At a turn in the corridor, a large model of an early biplane hung from the ceiling, and in an alcove, a life-size inflated gorilla wearing a bra and a tutu sat on a swivel chair. Two young men came walking toward me, and one stopped.

"Mr. Transit?" I knew him.

"Hello, Jonathan."

Jonathan Coolidge had interned at my agency two summers before, and when we couldn't take him on full time after his graduation, I'd sent him over to Pete, who hired him.

"How are you?" he asked.

"Okay. Things working out?"

"Sure."

Jonathan had an eager young face, acne, wire-rimmed glasses. "You were right," he went on. "It's a terrific shop, just as you said it would be."

"Glad you're happy. What're you working on?"

"Package goods mostly. TV stuff. Congratulations on Mercedes, by the way."

"Thanks."

Pete stepped out of his corner office to greet me. Pete was my age, tall, open-faced, tan. He had an athlete's balance and an executive's mind. He had been a great account executive and now ran his agency with deft control and a laissez-faire grace that concealed his competitiveness and ambition. He was wearing tailored gray slacks, a pale-yellow cotton shirt, a gold and gray Hermès tie, and black loafers. We went into his office and sat on opposite ends of his leather couch.

"Great going on Mercedes, fella," he said. "I had you picked all the way. I'm also jealous as shit."

"I'm just glad you didn't pitch it."

"Hell, I wasn't invited."

I gave Pete a look.

"So what's going on?" he asked.

"Yesterday morning, in Grand Central, I came face-to-face with Emily."

"Name I haven't heard in one long time, partner."

"Right."

"So tell me."

"She's a homeless person."

"What?"

"Street person, swear to God."

Pete's speakerphone buzzed; his secretary cut in: "Ben Brassie on the line. Want it?"

"No, and no more calls, please."

"There's more," I said. "A daughter."

"Whose daughter?"

"Mine."

"You don't have a daughter."

"Seems I do. Met her yesterday."

Something with impact came up by way of my throat and stopped behind my nose. I wasn't ready for this and did not want it. A show of emotion in this way now and in this place was abhorrent to me.

"How do you know she's yours?"

"She looks like me."

"That's not proof."

"Call it intuition."

It hit. Liquid, across my eyes, into my nostrils.

"I thought Emily was gone, *that* was gone, that part of me was gone. She . . . the way she looked . . . *old* — plus, she's sick."

Pete was squinting at me, as into a hard wind.

"Sick how?"

I waved his question off, and it all came to a peak, and I was speaking from a place in me I had forgotten: "She was beautiful. Pete, you remember. And it's my fault, gotta be, Christ, out there in rags, her mind bent in half, talks nonsense half the time, she's like from another world, some dark place that'll burn your brain, and here I am . . ." Twenty years of ignorance and neglect froze my face into a mask, and my vulnerability and feeling and mode of expression embarrassed me deeply.

Pete had gone pale. He licked his lips. "Emily was erratic, right? The drugs she did. And I hope you're not forgetting who left who?"

"She left me because she had to, given who she was. When I met her I was one thing, and then I changed."

"We all change."

"But artists don't. True artists don't!"

"Oh come on. You think you're to blame? For what she is now? Bullshit."

His phrase was like a slap. "Long and short is, I have to find her again."

"Think you can help her?"

"Or she can help me . . . ."

He was exasperated. "How?"

"Pete, we sell, we buy. But what do we keep?"

Pete's phone buzzed again. "I'm awfully sorry, Peter. If you're going to make your lunch . . ."

I nodded at him and said: "Let me go. Really." Not that I had anywhere to go.

He said to his secretary: "Three minutes."

"I'm talking about values, Pete. I was going to be a poet. I didn't become one." I spread my arms wide. "I became this. And what do I have that counts?"

"One hell of a good goddamn life, for openers." He stood. "Listen, yes, this is a shock, no question. But what are you doing? Questioning your whole life? What for?"

I took a breath. "I broke off with Mary last night."

"Why?"

"She wanted me to commit and I don't know what the word means."

"This was before or after you saw Emily?"

"Before."

Pete squinted again, as if I were ever more difficult to see. "What are you going to tell me next? The two things are related?"

"If you can't love, bad things happen."

There was silence, and I knew he was out of time. I said: "So your advice to me is what? Walk away from her?"

"No. Do what your conscience tells you. But run yourself down? Because you cashed in the fifth-floor walkup and threadbare life for something better? No, no. That gets you nowhere. So listen, come on over to the apartment tonight. Beth and I will do up something — our famous sea bass, whatever. Or you and I can go out pub crawling, or just do nothing. How about it?"

I have no idea how I answered.

***

Out in the corridor, I headed back to the reception area. Jonathan was leaning against a desk. He obviously wanted to talk, but I kept walking, hoping he'd change his mind. He didn't.

"You know," he said, falling in step with me, "we had a pool going on who'd get Mercedes. I think Mr. Fleming wanted to pitch it but held off." Jonathan's words were irritating background noise. "Not that we'd have beaten you guys. He knew you'd get it."

I was near the exit. *Just let me get out of here.* Jonathan rambled on: "What he said was, `You don't need any oracle to know who'll win that account.'"

I stopped and took Jonathan by the arm. "Who said that?"

"Pete — Mr. Fleming."

His face swam in front of me.

I pronounced the word carefully: "Oracle?"

Jonathan eyed me curiously. "Sure."

"Jonathan, you got a phone I can use?" He led me to his office, a cubicle smaller than Tom Blackwell's. I dialed; Tom picked up.

"Tom — Jack."

"Yo."

"When people went to oracles, how did it . . . what was the deal, exactly?"

"When they went to what?"

"Oracles."

"Chief, come on — I gotta start charging you for this stuff."

"Just tell me. How did it work?"

"Depended on the oracle. At Delphi, you were ushered into the presence of a priestess in a cave."

"Who ushered you?"

"One of her attendants."

"Then what?"

"She went into a trance and answered questions. The trance was caused by vapor rising from a cleft in the rocks."

"That's it?"

"What do you want already, a musical with a rotating set?"

"Could she find missing persons?"

"In a pinch, probably."

I thanked Tom, hung up, thanked Jonathan, and got out of there.

Eight

I got to Grand Central in ten minutes. No music, no Emily. In the waiting room, however, sat the old lady in the New York Giants sweatshirt. Next to her was the middle-aged man with the shopping bags. There was a lot wrong with his face. Next to him was the well-dressed young man. Less well-dressed today, he wore a scruffy-looking leather jacket, though his pants were clean and pressed.

Marvin was not there.

I sat down next to the man in the nice pants. "Where's Marvin?"

"Are you his lawyer?"

"No."

"I'm under instructions to only speak to his lawyer."

The old woman leaned forward. "To speak only to his lawyer."

"That's what I said."

"No, you said to only speak to his lawyer. Adverb `only´ in wrong place."

The man looked confused. I spoke to the old lady: "Do you know where I can find Marvin?"

She took a long time to think about this. "No."

The man with the shopping bags stirred. "Why don't you ask me?" He produced a bottle from somewhere. Thunderbird, nearly empty. He unscrewed the top and drank.

I squatted on my haunches in front of him. It was his nose that was wrong — it was smashed nearly flat, a mass of flesh and dried blood. I tried to look into his eyes and ignore his nose. It wasn't possible.

"What's your name?"

"Who's askin'?"

"I'm Jack Transit."

"You run the subways?"

"No. You are . . . ?"

"I are fucked up."

"What happened to your nose, if I may ask?"

"You may not."

"The old one was worse," said the young man in the leather jacket. "Didn't really suit him. Didn't properly reflect his personality."

"There's truth in that," said the drinking man.

"Okay," I said. "Tell me, what's your name?"

"Burt. And this here's Jim. And this lady here is Mrs. Jenkins, who once taught school."

I looked from one to the other. "I'm pleased to meet all of you."

"What's changed?" asked the young man. I did not get his meaning. "Yesterday you weren't especially glad to meet us. What changed?"

"I guess I did." Silence. "Burt," I said. "I knew a Burt in high school. Burt Wheelock — good baseball player."

Burt's eyes ceased focusing, then focused again. "Don't know him."

"Hell of a good shortstop."

"I played right field."

"Your size, you could probably hit."

"I hit some long balls." Burt approached speaking the way a crocodile wrestler might approach a crocodile. With extreme caution and control. "Senior year I batted two ninety."

— 59 —

"Burt," I said, "I'm trying really hard to find someone. I'm trying to find Emily, the flute player."

"Plays a fine flute."

"Do you know where she is?"

"No."

"Well," I said, "yesterday Marvin told me there is someone who knows where Emily is. He called it . . . this person, the oracle."

"Marvin has his own ideas," said Burt.

"You ever hear of an oracle?"

"No."

"Okay, do you know where Marvin is, then?"

"Now?"

"Yes."

"God damn!" He suddenly held the bottle up. "I just started this sucker this morning, and now she's dead. Who's got a drink?"

No one answered.

"Parties ain't what they used to be." He waved the bottle back and forth. "You like to booze, Mr. Transit?"

"Call me Jack. A little. Just social drinking."

"What the hell do you think this is? The worst part of being dry is that it parches you out. Particularly, it parches out one part of you bad."

"What part is that, Burt?"

"The memory."

"Uh-huh."

"Your memory for people and their whereabouts."

"Burt, if I were to go on a little errand, such as to the liquor store, and bring you back some Thunderbird, you'd still be here when I got back, wouldn't you?"

"An earthquake wouldn't move me."

"Good. Maybe a new bottle will water your memory a little."

"That could happen."

"Your memory, say, of where Marvin is."

He smiled and nodded.

As I got up, Mrs. Jenkins laughed.

I found a liquor store on Lexington. When I got back with the wine, only the two men were there. I handed the bottle to Burt.

"Well, ain't that somethin'." He broke the seal, twisted the cap off, and held the bottle to his nose. "That's my brew." He took a long drink, wiped his lips. "Know what tonight is? Halloween. Watch yourself on the streets. Things can happen."

"Would this be a good time to tell me where Emily is?"

"Whoa, wait, no. I can't tell you that. Marvin — I can tell you where *he* is. That's all."

"I hoped you could tell me about Emily."

"No sir."

Jesus, I'm being had. I counted to five, slowly.

"Okay, tell me where Marvin is."

"I believe you will find him at this hour working one of two places: the token booth downstairs, or the money machines over at Chemical."

"The IRT downstairs?" I said. "And the Chemical bank where?"

"Forty-second and whatever . . . Lexington." As I moved away, I said back over my shoulder: "Burt, do me a favor and have that nose looked at."

He said after me: "What for?"

***

Marvin stood at the IRT token booth downstairs, turban in place, in his right gloved hand a paper cup. People were in line at the booth. A lady in a designer beige coat, with black-rimmed glasses hanging from a gold lanyard, took her token, stepped past Marvin.

"Anything you can spare?" he asked. "Court case coming up."

She looked at him hard with unflinching pale-blue eyes. "What?"

"Anything you can spare? Court case —"

"Absolutely not."

"You sure?"
She walked by.
"Thanks anyway."
I approached him.
"Marvin."
"Aha," he said. "The man in the gray flannel mind."
I moved him away from the booth. The lady in the coat went through the turnstile. "I like her," said Marvin, nodding toward the woman. "She knows her own heart."
"She turned you down."
"That's the downside, certainly." His lips parted, half grimace, half smile, showing his pointed front teeth.
We were beside the floor-to-ceiling bars that extend from the turnstiles to the wall.
"I'm still looking for Emily." He tilted his head to listen. "You mentioned an oracle."
"Just now?"
"Earlier."
"You want to see her?"
"The oracle? Yes, if it'll lead me to Emily."
"Ready to pay?" he asked.
"Maybe. How much?"
"You give me your credit card. I buy as much as I can with it in six hours."
"Forget it."
"Wait now. Observe me and ask yourself — how many places are going to let me use it, even let me in? Stores? Restaurants? Travel agents? Car whadayacallits — dealerships? I probably won't be able to buy a thing. May not cost you a cent."
"No, thanks."
"Sorry, then."
"What about the flat fee deal. That's what you said yesterday."
"That was a one-day special."
"Look, damn it. I want to see Emily. She's my ex-wife. It's very, very important. Now talk to me."
"Oracle points you to her. Requires plastic."

"Well fuck you, you fucking demented —" I walked away, back up the stairs. My head was throbbing, my teeth clenched. I hurried for ten or twelve steps, slowed, stopped. Stood there for a long moment, went back. Marvin was where I'd left him, staring down at his hand.

"I'm back."

His face was flushed, his narrow eyes pained.

I calculated what I needed to say. "Sorry about just now. Didn't mean it."

"No, I'm sorry. For being a hardass. I have to be, rules being rules."

I looked at him for a long moment, took out my wallet, flipped it open to the little clear plastic holders, in one of which was my American Express card. I showed it to him.

"I only take MasterCard."

I held his eyes, flipped the plastic holders over so my MasterCard showed.

"What's the expiration date on that?"

I showed him.

"Okay."

I took the card from my wallet. "Listen to me. You rip me off, I'll go ballistic. Do you understand me?"

He nodded.

"If you're fucking with me, I'll make you very sorry."

Another nod, and a thin smile.

"Now tell me exactly how this works."

Nine

*H*e led the way to the Times Square shuttle. The train was there, doors open, receiving passengers. We walked past it, to a concrete wall at the station's far end. A metal door. Marvin glanced back once, pulled the door handle, let me go ahead of him. A stairway. We went down, turned left, descended another stairway, entered a small room, off which was a door marked HIGH VOLTAGE. We went past this door, turned right. Here the walls suddenly shook as an unseen train passed nearby, its steel wheels screaming on iron tracks. We edged along a narrow walkway and then went down another stairway. Then through a long, poorly lit passageway and into a low-ceilinged open space with naked low-wattage bulbs overhead. It was cool and dry. A cement wall ran forty or fifty feet along one side. Pylons had been driven into the wall, and clothesline had been strung from them to three wrapped steampipes, which ran parallel to the wall about fifteen feet from it. Sheets and clothes hung on these lines, providing improvised partitions. Within spaces thus formed lived groups of people. In the one nearest to me, a pale, thin man lay asleep on a green army blanket. Next to him slept a small woman and near them a child of about two played with a Betty Boop doll. I walked alongside the wall, poking through the dividers. Marvin came after me, put a hand on my arm. "Not the neighborhood we're looking for."

"Let me go."

I pushed aside a fabric wall of tie-dyed shirts and scarves. A five-by-five cubicle with red, yellow, and black tie-dyed walls and floor. Facing me, a stocky, bearded man sitting in a large yellow easy chair, reading *The New York Times*. The paper was two months out of date. The man hissed at me, pulled the paper closer to his face. Marvin pulled me back.

"She's not here; she never comes here. Come on."

We left that place, went down another cement stairway. The smell of sulfur, and humidity rising. I removed my overcoat and loosened my necktie. Almost total darkness. Down another staircase, the last steps of which were slippery. Total silence. We moved along a narrow concrete corridor, stepped through a low door. I heard water dripping. Then we were standing on a wooden catwalk, a foot below which was moving water.

"This way." Marvin led me along the catwalk — it was very dark now, and we had to duck because the ceiling angled down — and after a couple dozen steps a light appeared in the distance. The ceiling rose just before the spot where this light was.

We moved along the catwalk and came to an arched entry, beyond which was the source of light. The arch was quite high, eight feet or so, and I saw that it had graffiti on it, two tiers of yellow and purple foot-high ornate letters. On top, a capital *K* followed by three letters, a capital *W* followed by two letters. Below that, a capital *Y* followed by two letters, a capital *A* followed by two letters.

I had to work to make it out.

Know Who
You Are

I became aware of a new sound, a subtle hissing. Marvin put a hand on my shoulder. "I don't go further."

"Meaning what?"

"She'll be in there. You're on your own."

It was very humid now. My shirt stuck to my sides, my clothes felt heavy, confining. I handed my overcoat to Marvin.

"So the deal is I just go on in?"

"If you wish."

"Then what?"

"Present your question."

I peered in under the arch, trying to figure out the light, and saw that, about ten feet in, steam rose from below the catwalk, disappearing somewhere past the top of the arch.

"Where will you be?" I asked.

Marvin didn't answer. I turned. He wasn't there. The catwalk stretched back the way we'd come, into total darkness, empty. It was intensely quiet, except for the hissing of the steam beyond the arch. I removed my sports jacket and laid it on the catwalk, moved closer to the arch, touched it. The cement was cool. I took a breath and stepped through.

I was again on a cement walkway, which sloped downward at an angle of perhaps fifteen degrees. Six feet ahead of me the steam spewed steadily upward. I couldn't see its source. A steel-mesh ceiling, eight feet high. The steam escaped through it behind the arch. I could take just one more step forward without being scalded, and I did this. The passageway opened out to the left. On the wall, in the same colors and style as the letters above the arch, was a thick arrow, pointing ahead.

I moved cautiously along, rounding the column of steam, and what I saw stopped me. Twenty feet ahead was Ronald Reagan — or rather, Ronald Reagan's face: a painted rubber mask, propped on a stick. His quizzical smile, dark-brown hair, a youthful hairline. Alongside it, on sticks, were two more masks: Charlie Chaplin and Jimmy Stewart. Immediately behind these was a four-foot-high yellow curtain, the bottom swaying slightly, in a draft. I was angry at being startled, and the anger spoke.

"Cute! Anyone home?"

A muffled female voice came from behind the curtain:

> Jack Alan Transit, aged forty-five.
> Born in Jamestown, New York,
> resides West Seventy-sixth Street.
> Senior vice-president, Greenberg Transit Fulsome.
> Here in the matter of Emily LeMoine Transit.

The voice was husky. A hand appeared on the right side of the curtain, pulled it aside. Sitting on a raised platform, wearing a yellow cotton poncho, was Marilyn Monroe. The long, synthetic white-blond hair, the mouth with bright-red lips set in a knowing smile, the oversized beauty mark on her cheek. It was another mask, this one adorning a living figure. And Marilyn wasn't alone. No, no. Propped on a stick at her right was Howdy Doody, and on her left, the Frankenstein monster.

Marilyn spoke.

> Approach.

I didn't move.

> No one forced you to come here.
> Do you choose to stay?

I nodded.

> Then the oracle of oracles greets you.
> Trial and tenacity mark the path
> to knowledge.
> Fear must be overcome
> and marketplace skills rendered superfluous.

I tried to see through the eye slits of the mask, to spot human eyes, but there was only darkness there. I drifted closer. The poncho was a cheap piece of fabric with a hole cut out for the head. Her hands were out of sight beneath it, and jutting from the bottom of it was the badly scuffed toe of a running shoe.

"So now what?" I asked.

> State what you've come for.

"Some answers."

> Three questions are permitted.

"Who the hell are you?"

> One whose name is written on celluloid,
> whose body has known the seven violations,
> and whose words resemble truth.

I snickered. "Resemble truth? No, no, I want the real thing, thanks."

> Truth is before words,
> the way blood and water are before birth.
> Ask your second question.

"Wait, I get only three questions?"

> Didn't I say so?
> And you just asked your second,
> leaving one.

"Hold it, no, slow down, don't count that one. It was rhetorical — just for information." She tilted toward me and cocked her head to one side. When she spoke, a hardness was in her voice.

> You are a man with an attitude of
> irreverence, and your tongue has spoken
> twice with no connection to your heart.
> Fortunately for you, mine never does.
> Tell me, why should I ease the burden of your error?

Suddenly I was breathing deeply, from the diaphragm. Something moved in my blood, a shiver.

"I'm sorry. I'm out of my milieu here. I need two more questions. Please."

She neither moved nor spoke. I chose to take that as assent.

"Tell me where I can find Emily."

> Clear your mind, then, and listen.
> Contemplate twenty-six plus fifty-three.
> Start where rocks turn to gold,
> angle across to the animal kingdom,
> skip to what grows in Flanders fields,
> pass under a white trumpet to stained glass times ten,
> and find her where love has pitched his mansion.

A riddle! I should have been ready for it.

Well, professional skills *do* count. I went over it three times slowly, and I had it memorized. Marilyn sat on her perch, attended by her masks.

One question left.

I was ready. "Where's Minerva?"
She was very quick with the reply:

> Devil, devil, first,
> snowman, ditto,
> nothing, nothing.

I waited to see if there was more.
"How do I know this is legitimate? Not a con game?"

That's another question.

"Just tell me!"
She stood up abruptly, a hand came out from under the poncho, and she pointed at me.

> You're a fool if you think
> you issue orders here!

Christ, the chill again! It disconcerted me, because all around was heat and humidity. I heard hard breathing whistle in and out of the mask's mouth, and for the first time I saw eyes behind the slits.

> How long will you allow your arrogance to defeat you?

She's not going to break me! My mind swirled now, I couldn't focus. My legs felt weak, but I would stand here, stand and not show it.
"I want another question, but that wasn't it. Give me another question. Please."
She was still for a second.

> Ask it.

The chill was an ice storm, born of some shattering of an internal thermostat. Before I knew it, I was at the level of her knee. I had dropped to my knees. I had knelt down. I had never done that before, anywhere. I looked up at her. What I wanted to ask came onto my tongue hard and cold.
"I once was a poet, and wanted only one thing. To mine from the deepest part of myself what was most precious and from this to write poems beautiful enough to make people look inward in wonder. I wanted every day to pinpoint the exact place where life

is a miracle, and exult in that. But I had no real belief in myself. What I had was a partner — Emily. She believed in me. I tried to live on her belief, but couldn't. I got tired. So I took my skill with words and entered the marketplace, sold it to the highest bidder. For this she left me. Said she could not love the Jack who was not the poet. I didn't feel a thing; refused to feel a thing, because to feel it would be death. Of course my poetry dried up. But now . . . I want to feel it now — feel my life."

What's stopping you?

"Emily rejects me. And there's a daughter, Minerva, and she rejects me. I have to find Emily, find Minerva; have to have them, know them."

I gave you the keys to finding them.

I screamed: "I want more!" It came ripping out of me, phlegm following.

Now my palms joined my knees on the cement, which was cool and rough on my skin. Behind me the hiss of steam and somewhere far away perhaps the rumble of a train, though it could have been nothing, just the meaningless noise within the awful silence.

I shouted it all out, holding nothing back:

"Am I a poet? Can I recapture that? If not, who in the hell am I? If not, what use am I? What's going to happen to me?"

> One question becomes four,
> and I'll address the last only.
> You will encounter four things:
> death under a horse's belly,
> a gift worth having,
> a motorcycle heading south,
> and after that, the sunrise.

"Who am I?"

>Any answer I give to that
>would be unsatisfactory.
>Any answer you find,
>provided it follows honest work,
>will be true.

>And so we're finished. Go the way you came.

 I found my sports jacket where I'd put it, and hurried along the wooden slats of the passageway. Somewhere, on one of the stairs, Marvin appeared, with my overcoat. I took it and brushed by him, finally emerging into daylight. I moved through the station again, up more stairs and out, and was hit with the cold autumn air . . . and the bright sunlight. Vanderbilt Avenue. I stood by a light pole, a hand on it for support, and suddenly there was an awful roar, as three taxis came barreling along past me, yellow hooded monsters in a pack. I jumped back, the shock of this mechanized chaos making breath catch in my throat. Then panting, exhausted, throat raw, a headache pounding, I turned and walked north. Everything was too loud, too jangling, as if I'd never been here before. The city was a monster that could swallow me whole. I stopped once to breathe, then continued. After a few blocks I stopped abruptly, took out a pen, fumbled in my pocket for a notebook, and wrote down what she'd said to me. The riddles first, then the rest. I had an awful fear someone I knew would come along and interrupt me, and I'd forget.

 When I finished, I carefully tucked the notebook away. My choices were to go left to Madison Avenue or right to Park. I couldn't stand the thought of the former, the street where I'd spent twenty years, poured out my liver and brains and spleen in pursuit of a better phrase. Somewhere under that black asphalt were buried my heart, my memory, my unwritten poems. So I went over to Park, and passing people in expensive clothes, with expensive faces, I held my head up, let the cold light come at me off glass towers, and kept walking north.

Ten

*I*t was colder. As I walked a chill went through my clothes and into skin, muscle, bone. I was hungry. At Fifty-fourth Street I turned toward Lexington Avenue and found a coffee shop. It was clean, light, two-thirds empty, lunchtime being about over. I picked a table away from other customers, left my coat on, huddled there. I opened the plastic-covered menu.
"What'll it be, hon?"
I looked up. A waitress bending near me — horror! — *wearing a mask*. I clutched the edge of the table.
Her eyebrows and mouth moved.
"Everything okay, doll?"
I probably nodded.
"You sure?"
"Yes."
It wasn't a mask; it was a face. Everything about it was aged except the cumulative effect, which conveyed youth — or a caricature thereof. A fetching smile, around which puckered aging skin. Narrow, expressive eyes, too deepset. Long cheeks going soft. The face of a little girl who'd gotten old and was shocked by it. She could have been twenty-one going on forty-five, or twenty-six going on fifty. She wore a name tag that said SALLY.

"The special of the day is lasagna and a house salad, comes with coffee. Very good."

"I want hot soup."

"Soup of the day is chicken noodle. Very good. I had some myself."

"And it's very hot?"

"Of course."

I ordered the soup and a tuna sandwich; she smiled and went away. She had thin ankles and a little girl's tight rear end, and she listed slightly to the right, sign of a bad back. I could sustain no interest in her, or in anything else. I felt an immense resistance to thinking. I wanted either to sleep or to go somewhere warm. I forced myself to take out my notebook.

Emily's riddle. Twenty-six plus fifty-three is seventy-nine. The year? Someone's age? A street reference — Seventy-ninth Street? Might be. "Rocks turn to gold" meant nothing . . . but "animal kingdom": that could be the zoo! Central Park. "White trumpet" came up empty, but I thought "love has pitched his mansion" had a ring to it. A line from something.

I'd go into the park at Seventy-ninth Street and see what rocks I passed. Turn to gold . . . maybe when the sun hits them. That would be a function of the time of day. Anything about time here? "Stained glass times ten" — a time reference?

"What grows in Flanders fields." Poppies, of course, from the poem. In Flanders fields the poppies grow, et cetera. So I'll look for poppies growing near a rock the sun hits at ten o'clock, and that should lead me to the zoo. Or I could just start at the zoo and look for the white trumpet. Or I could forget all that and just find where homeless people hang out near the zoo, and start looking, start asking.

"Here's your soup." The waitress set a large bowl in front of me. Steam rose from broth crammed with vegetables and pieces of white chicken meat. The soup smelled good, and I spooned up a small amount. Nearly too hot to eat.

Hell, the whole thing could have been an elaborate scam to get my credit card. In which case it's a classic. Have to write it up, send it to *New York* magazine. More important, I have to call and get the card canceled. Only if it's a lark, though. But if it isn't? There's a bind.

"Here we go doll." Sally arrived with a tuna sandwich.

"Thanks."

"What's to drink?"

"Diet Coke, lemon."

She left.

I continued eating the soup, finished it, ate half the sandwich. Now for Minerva. I'd written:

Devil, devil, first,
snowman, ditto,
nothing, nothing.

Not a lot of geography there. Devil. Halloween reference? A mask of some kind. Snowman is an eight in golf. Two snowmen equals sixteen. Sixteenth Street? A store that sells Halloween masks on Sixteenth Street? I could check the yellow pages.

Sally brought my Coke, and I sipped it and ate the other half of my sandwich. I looked through the window at the cabs and cars and trucks and buses, then I felt Sally at my shoulder.

"How was everything, doll?"

"Very good."

"I'm glad." She picked up my empty soup bowl and plate. "Coffee?"

"Sure."

"It's fresh. You'll like it. Dessert?"

"No, thanks."

"Not apple pie? Fresh made."

"No; no, thanks."

"Okay, doll. You just relax and I'll bring coffee, though I have to ask, did something memorable just happen to you?"

I can't imagine how I must have looked at her.

"Don't mean to pry. Sorry."

"No; but why do you ask that?"

"I'm psychic. I see auras."

"What do you see?"

"You're in distress, a kind you never experienced before. But it's not all negative. It can lead you to your goal."

I reached out a hand and took her free wrist.

"Do you read riddles?"

"Depends."

I moved my open notebook toward her and as she glanced at it she took something from her apron pocket and handed it to me. A business card.

> Sister Sally.
> Tarot. Palm readings. Future.
> No problem too small.
> 60 West Eighty-fifth St.
> New York, N.Y. 10024

"That's you? Sister Sally?"

"Yes. Appointments start at six. Come see me."

"I've got no time for a scam."

"You're frightened, desperate. I can help you. For example, did you know that in numerology, the devil's number is six? Think about it." She turned and walked away. I stared at Minerva's riddle.

> Devil, devil, first, snowman, ditto, nothing, nothing.
> Six, six, first, snowman, ditto, nothing, nothing.
> Six, six, first, eight, eight, nothing, nothing.
> Six, six, one, eight, eight, zero, zero!

A phone number. A goddamn phone number! I closed the notebook and stood up. A pay phone was on the wall just past the entrance. I walked that way. Coming at me with my check was Sally. I whispered, "Don't go anywhere." Then I was at the phone, reaching to my pocket for a quarter.

I dropped the quarter in the slot and listened for the dial tone. My lips were dry. I licked them once, twice, then slowly pushed each touchtone square in sequence: six, six again, on up to the one, the eight twice, the zero, and then I waited, waited, and hung up the phone. A metallic tinkle as my quarter dropped into the return.

Coward!

Think. See: an athlete's stride. Her running away from me across the floor of Grand Central. Running across Forty-fifth Street, away from me. *Take the chance.* I have a number to dial, I have something to say. I have something to say.

I fished the quarter out of the return, stared at the phone, at those touchtone numbers, cold, digits enameled into metal, keys to kingdoms, coveted codes to living rooms, bedrooms, offices, modems, computers, fax machines, security systems, homes; access to wires over which words travel, words find you, hurt you, heal you, change you. Devil, devil, first, snowman, snowman, zero, zero . . . . Two rings. A male voice: "Star Four." Background noise, voices.

"I'm calling for Minerva LeMoine."

"Hold on." Sound of phone receiver set down, voices, a kind of tinny music, laughter. Then:

"Hello." It was her.

"Minerva, it's your father, and before you hang up, I'm calling because I'm trying to find Emily, to help her. She's missing — do you know where she is?"

A silence so abrupt I thought she had hung up, but background noises said she hadn't.

"How missing?"

"She's not in Grand Central. Her people there don't know where she is."

"What a joke! Of course they do: they just aren't telling you. What do you want with her anyway?"

"To help her. Get her off the street."

"Well forget it. She is off the street."

"Where is she? Please tell me."

"Where people like you can't get at her. Now go back to your life, where you belong. And how the fuck did you get this number?"

"Don't talk to me that way. I love you."

A profound silence: mine from my own shock at what I'd said; hers from who knows what?

And then real silence. She'd hung up.

***

Sally looked at me from a table she was clearing, and I hurried to her. "You solved that riddle. Now I have another one."

Along the length of her arm she was balancing two dirty plates with silverware, two water glasses, two half-filled coffee cups, and two saucers.

"Not now. I have an opening tonight at seven. At the address on my card."

I snapped: "I don't have that kind of time."

She pursed her lips. "Tonight at seven."

She headed toward the kitchen. I considered going after her, but didn't. I grabbed my check off the table, threw down a tip, snared my topcoat, paid at the register. Outside I hailed a cab.

"The zoo," I said to the driver.

"The what?"

"The zoo in Central Park."

On the ride uptown I reflected on what I'd said to Minerva: I love you. Had I meant it? How could I? I didn't even know her.

At Fifth and Sixty-fourth I paid the cabbie and walked down the wide steps to the zoo. Suddenly I was light-headed. I put out a hand to steady myself and leaned against the building. This was what . . . ? Exhaustion? Anxiety? I was no longer cold. Overheated, in fact. I loosened my tie.

"You okay, mister?"

The small voice of a small boy. A round face with large blue eyes. A New York Mets hat, orange shirt, clashing red-and-yellow bandanna, stiff new blue jeans, matching new blue denim jacket with shiny buttons. He was seven, eight. "See the polar bear yet?"

I shook my head.

"You gotta see it. Swims over an' back, over an' back, on his back and on his stomach, all day long. You can stand behind this big piece of glass and see him. No one could swim all day long like that, not even Jordan. Plus he's huge. This big." He held his hands wide.

"Who's Jordan?" I asked.

"My brother, who's on the swim team. I keep tellin' him to come over an' see the bear if he wants to see real swimming. But he don't come."

"Christopher!"

A woman wheeling a baby carriage came toward us. "Christopher, come here." She took his hand, eyed me oddly, tugged him away from me.

I walked along the black, four-foot-high iron-rod fence. People were sitting on benches near the seal pond. Beyond them I could see other people at the African monkey compound. Past that would be where the polar bear was. A tall, lean man in a Department of Parks uniform was approaching. The name NAT was embroidered on his jacket pocket.

"Excuse me," I said. "Is there an area of the zoo with stained glass?"

"With what?"

"Stained glass. Any of the buildings have stained-glass windows?"

He had a high forehead and receding hairline, faint pockmarks in the hollows of his cheeks, a small silver ring in his left earlobe.

"This is a zoo, not a church."

"I know it's a zoo."

He started moving on. I stepped after him. "Is there a place nearby where homeless people hang out? Where they sleep?"

"Absolutely not."

"Because I'm looking for someone. A woman. Five seven, over forty, wears a —"

"We keep 'em the hell away from here —"

" — knit cap, plays a flute."

"Men, women, don't matter, they got no business near the zoo. Can't have them bothering the animals or the people. This is a city-run facility."

"Well, where's the nearest place in the park where they might be?"

He leaned toward me, his face intense. He spoke quietly, conspiratorially. "See, your basic homeless person — and I'm as sympathetic as the next person — wants to be on the street. And that's the truth. It's not a question of what they can or cannot do. It's beyond that . . . it's what that individual has or has not been exposed to, his or her life experience which drains a kind of desire to be what you might call upstanding. I've worked here twelve years, be thirteen November ninth. Seen the changes — the attitudes change, the landscape, everything. Question of pride: how people treat themselves is how they'll be treated."

Something in me ignited, a distant flare. I turned away.

"As for where you might look, Bethesda Fountain is your best bet. All the lowlifes are there — thick as thieves up there. Thick as rats."

In a flash I had turned, grabbed him by his shirt, pushed him up against the fence. I must have been pushing against his larynx, because he spoke in a high, stifled voice, like a cartoon character.

"Let me the fuck go!"

"You ignorant son of a bitch!"

"Let me go!" He moved, his shoulder dropping, forearm coming up.

A bomb went off in my stomach. Pain mushroomed out and up, somewhere there was a gurgling, and I was on one knee and one hand, the knee on concrete, the hand on grass, wondering if I was going to die. I tried to breathe, failed, tried again; I was suffocating. Only then did I realize I'd been punched. I couldn't see anything — the world was blackness and fireflies. Somewhere high over me came his voice.

"Motherfucker, think you can come in here and rough me up."

The smell of rage in my nostrils. The sounds of percussion

instruments in my ears. I crawled off the walkway onto the grass. Time stood still, sped up, downshifted, went backwards. I was breathing finally, in small, noisy fits.

"You gonna barf?" A small, high voice.

Staring down at me was Christopher. I sat up. The man in the uniform was gone. I shook my head.

"He bashed you good. Wham! You went down."

"Yes."

"I know his name if you want to report him."

From behind him, his mother appeared, grabbed his arm. He dug the toes of his sneakers into the grass. He tried to whisper into my ear, but it came as more of a breathy shout:

"Go ahead, barf," he said. "You always feel better after."

Eleven

I walked north out of the zoo. Every twenty steps or so, I had to stop. I could breathe only shallowly, because of the pain. Soon I came to a bridge underpass. Off on the grass I saw two large cardboard boxes, each big enough for a person to sleep in. No one was inside. One contained four or five ragged pieces of clothing and a copy of *Reader's Digest*. I kept walking and came eventually to the Mall, then headed toward the Bethesda Fountain. A few people were strolling near the fountain and down along the lake. They were distant and strange, like members of some other race. It was cold here, and the water looked rough and repellent. I didn't see any sign of homeless people, so I just quit. I was on a losing mission. I wasn't making use of the riddle. I would never find Emily.

At the roadway above the fountain, I got a taxi and gave the driver my address. I slumped back in the seat, felt under my rib cage. It was sore and still hurt when I breathed.

At home, I stood in my kitchen staring into the refrigerator. I opened a bottle of flavored seltzer and took a drink. In the living room, I lay down on the couch. I lay there a long time. After a while I sat up.

. . . skip to what grows in Flanders fields,
pass under a white trumpet to stained glass times ten,
and find her where love has pitched his mansion.

Love has pitched his mansion. I went to my bookshelf. Translation of something? No. I scanned my poetry shelf. Yeats. I took down his *Collected Poems*, scanned titles, and there it was, the fourth in the Crazy Jane group: "Crazy Jane Talks with the Bishop."

I met the Bishop on the road
And much said he and I.
"Those breasts are flat and fallen now
Those veins must soon be dry;
Live in a heavenly mansion,
Not in some foul sty."

"Fair and foul are near of kin,
And fair needs foul," I cried.
"My friends are gone, but that's a truth
Nor grave nor bed denied,
Learned in bodily lowliness
And in the heart's pride.

"A woman can be proud and stiff
When on love intent;
But Love has pitched his mansion in
The place of excrement;
For nothing can be sole or whole
That has not been rent."

The place of excrement. A public bathroom? Subway? Where's there stained glass in a subway? Maybe she's in a church after all; would correlate with the bishop thing. She's in a church with a bathroom. Which churches take in homeless people? Better look into that. Instead, I took Sally's card from my wallet. Seven o'clock, she'd said. It was now five-fifteen. Okay, I could wait. I'd have to. I coughed, pain shooting up my chest wall.

I went to the kitchen, filled a cup with water, put in a tea bag, placed the cup in the microwave, hit the button. I watched the cup, and the string and paper tag hanging down the side of it. All was still, though in there somewhere, beyond my ability to see, molecules were doing a violent dance through the cup, water, tea bag. Everything inside that oven was moving, changing, exploding. So why's it all appear so still? I wanted to see the change, the molecules racing. What good are eyes if they can't see what's happening in front of them? Pluck 'em out if they offend you. They offend me because they fail me. And my mind fails me, and my memory.

Hit the microwave's off button, open the door, take out the cup, remove the tea bag, take your tea, and go sit down. I raised the cup, let the orange-scented steam rise to my nose, felt a numinous balm. Then the cup, transmitter of the water's heat, scalded my lower lip. I smiled. The invisible molecules had done their work, and right on cue, they registered on my body as pain.

Too tired now. Must lie down. Must sleep . . . .

Me, naked. Below me, the river, my feet tethered firmly to the banks. Above me, something descending, rocketing down at me, dark wings tucked in, head extended toward me. Its beak is an instrument of death. Where will it hit, where pierce me? Head? Shoulder? Throat? I can't move, can't run. Can only put my hands up to fend off this horror. I do this, and scream.

I awoke to a screaming — a siren nearby, rupturing the night. I clutched my shoulders, my neck. I was alive.

***

Six-ten P.M. My half-drunk tea on the side table. Everything quiet. Then, again, the wailing siren. Police? Fire trucks? Ambulance?

The dream. Why this terror? That bird is what . . . ? Retribution? I decided to take a shower; went to my bathroom, stripped, turned on the water, looked down at the white enamel tub.

Burning candles on the side of the tub. The air sweet/sour with marijuana smoke, Emily in the tub, water to her waist. I stand, torn envelope in hand. I have a headache.

What's the matter? she says.

Nothing.

Come on.

The Midwest Review turned me down.

No.

I nod.

Bummer. Those are great poems you sent them. Your best yet. What do they know in the Midwest? You're in *Poetry*, for God's sake. And *Antaeus*, and *West Wind* . . . what else? You'll be in *The New Yorker* in a year, just watch.

Yeah.

Say it like you mean it.

She settles back into the bath, her moist hair wedded to her neck and shoulders.

I run my hand under the water, feeling the heat on my wrist. She removes from the soap dish the moist and burning joint, takes a hit, turns it toward me. Ease the pain, she says.

I shake my head.

Then try this. I've got news . . . of the good kind. The New York gig came through. Two concerts at the 92nd Street Y. That's August. And guess what in September?

I draw a blank.

Carnegie Hall.

I grasp her calf under the water. I kiss her. I didn't think it would come this soon, after what your agent said.

Later I make spaghetti, salad. We eat on the low table in the living room, drink Lancer's wine. Emily lights another joint, passes it to me. I take a hit, pass it back. She places it burning in an ashtray near her plate.

Emily?

What?

Idea. We move to New York.

No.

Why not?

Bad karma, she says.

Call Carnegie Hall bad karma?

Bad winters.

I frown.

New York scares me, she says.

Come on. It's definitely your next career move. You know the opportunities are there.

I have a dream about New York in which I'm freezing to death.

Nonsense.

We eat, drink.

You're not serious about New York, she says.

Yes.

You could write there?

I could work there. I want a job — a real job. I want to make money.

How?

Commercial. I could write commercially.

She sits forward, eyes wide.

What does that mean?

Advertising.

You're a poet! She gestures wildly, knocking her water glass over. The water spills onto the table, and into her ashtray, dousing the joint.

Later, in bed. She's far from me, against the wall.
Emily?
What?
You hate the idea that much?
How many people are born with your gift? Anyone can write advertising.
I'll still write poetry. But there's no money in it.
I'll make the money.
I'm not going to live off you. It's not a life for me.
She moves to me, her arms around me. She's cold, her feet frigid against my thighs, her hands chilled. She shakes against me.
Jesus, I say. Are you getting sick?
Hold me.
I do. Her lips to my ear. Don't sell out, please. It's death.

I showered, shaved, brushed my teeth. Put on winter-weight corduroys, ribbed Irish sweater, deck shoes. In my refrigerator I found a couple of half-full cartons of Chinese food. I stood in my kitchen, one foot up on the sink edge, and ate the food cold with chopsticks. Rinsed the bowl, threw on a blue wool jacket, went out onto West Seventy-sixth Street. It was dark now, and a raw, bitter wind was up. I hailed a cab.
The cabbie, a slim young bearded black man wearing a red and blue knitted cap, smiled and said: "Happy Halloween."
"Yeah, sure."
"Gotten cold."
"Very."
I gave him Sister Sally's address on West Eighty-fifth Street, and we started up Amsterdam.
"Already been trouble," said the cabbie, turning his radio down. "Some kids went berserk in a Gap in midtown."

Somewhere north of us more sirens. A fire truck swung into the intersection at Seventy-ninth Street.

"Now what the hell's this?" asked the cabbie.

Three or four fire trucks blocked the avenue to the north. Cars were stopping and honking. We edged left.

"Must be a damn fire."

"Street looks totally blocked," I said.

A lane opened ahead of us. "Take that," I said, "and turn over Seventy-ninth."

We squeezed past a parked car and gunned up along the opening. The light was green, and we turned left on Seventy-ninth.

The cabbie pointed to the sidewalk. "Check that out."

Just in from the corner were two people in gorilla suits. One suit was brown, one sort of bleached white. Behind them were kids in a line, all dressed for Halloween. A raccoon, a duck, a zebra, a ballerina, an astronaut.

"Yeah. Cute."

"Hey, you into crystals, man?" asked the cabbie.

"Not really."

"'Cause if you are, that's the place right there." He gestured toward where the Halloweeners were walking. An awning on a shabby-looking townhouse. "Best deals in town on rocks, man. Got your crystals, got your semiprecious stones, got whatever you want in minerals."

I craned my neck. On the awning it said: CRYSTAL ROCK GALLERY.

"Got stuff will cure you, help you relax, make you potent, make you mellow, cure backache — "

"Stop the cab!"

"What?"

"Stop the cab. Pull over."

He did. "What's the matter?"

"Nothing. I'm getting out." I gave him five dollars, pushed the door open and was out on the street.

Long shot? Maybe. Next to Crystal Rock Gallery a small sign said: SECOND FLOOR, GO RIGHT UP. Another sign posted hours, according to which the place was closed.

The opening of the riddle thrummed in my head:

> Contemplate twenty-six plus fifty-three.
> Start where rocks turn to gold . . .

If twenty-six plus fifty-three meant Seventy-ninth Street, then this shop fit the second line. A place to start. What's next?

> angle across to the animal kingdom.

To angle would be to cross the street again. I drifted east. A hair stylist. An antique store. A closed-up restaurant. At an angle across Seventy-ninth was a five-story apartment building, on the ground floor of which, above a window, in large aluminum letters, were the words ANIMAL HOSPITAL.

I stepped into the street, let traffic pass, including a van driven by a clown with an orange hat, next to whom sat Count Dracula, smoking a cigarette. Heavy metal music blared from the van's sound system. After crossing the street I stood staring at the animal hospital. A smaller sign said: M. RAPAL, VETERINARIAN. I looked at my watch. Seven after seven. I was late for Sister Sally. Next line?

> skip to what grows in Flanders fields . . .

Poppies. A flower store? None on this block. Must be Broadway. Of course: across, in the middle of the block going toward Eightieth Street, was a Korean deli, with cut flowers out front. I went to it. A small man in a huge sheepskin jacket squatted out front, trimming broccoli bunches, wrapping them in cellophane.

"Do you have poppies?" I asked
He looked up. "Poppies?"
"You know, flowers. Large red flowers. Poppies."
"No."
"Do you ever have them?"

"No. What you see. Nice mums, roses, snapdragons. Four dollars a bunch." I walked inside the store. A young Korean woman was behind the counter, wearing white cotton gloves with the fingertips cut out, ringing up groceries for a short man in an expensive topcoat.

I said to the woman: "Excuse me, do you ever have poppies?"
"Poppies?"
"Outside. Large red flowers."
"No poppies. Baby breath, tulip."
I turned to leave. Behind me the customer said to the woman: "Do you only have plain bagels?"
"Yes."
"No sesame, no —"
"No, just plain."

Out on the sidewalk, the smell of bagels wafted to me, not from the deli but from H&H, the bagel emporium on the corner of Eightieth.

It was useless. At the corner was a pay phone. I should call Sister Sally, apologize for being late, see if I could still come up. I had no change. Next to the deli was a candy and newspaper store, with an open window onto the street. I went over to get change. Coming at me out of H&H was a couple. The man was tall, blond, wore wire-rimmed glasses, a stylish black leather jacket, and a dark-blue cap; the woman was Japanese, in a gray cloth coat cut wide at the shoulders, carrying a briefcase in one hand, a paper bag in the other.

"What kind did you get?" asked the man.
"A plain, a raisin and two poppy."
They turned left on Eightieth. I stared after them.

Poppy. Poppy bagel. Of course that's not it; just coincidence. A tease, a bad joke. Dead end, period. I drifted to the corner and was looked vaguely after the couple. They walked close together, and the man had his arm around the woman's shoulder. I envied them.

Something caught my eye above them, white movement against a dark sky. It was a pigeon, and it landed on a casement of the building across the street. Below that, something else caught my eye. *Wait! What's the next line?*

   pass under a white trumpet . . .

   Waving in the breeze, supported by two poles, a two-story-high banner. A rich blue field on which was set block white lettering: ALL ANGELS' CHURCH. Below the letters, a white angel blowing into a long white trumpet.

   pass under a white trumpet to stained glass times ten,
   and find her where love has pitched his mansion.

   At the church, I went up stone steps to a heavy glass door with a brass handle. Embossed on a plastic shield was the word RING. On the doorframe, a bell button.
   I depressed it. A buzzer sounded. I entered. A slate-floored, high-ceilinged foyer, off which was a small office. From inside, a small, bright-eyed woman with high cheekbones and a prominent chin smiled at me. She wore a tailored blue dress and her hair was pulled back neatly into a bun.
   "Can I help you?"
   "I'm looking for someone. A homeless person. A woman, middle-aged, plays a flute. I thought she might be here."
   "And you are?"
   I gave her my name.
   "And this person is a family member?"
   "Yes."
   The woman shifted in her chair, reached up, and with a manicured hand removed a yellow pencil from her hair bun. I watched the pencil lead touch lightly the top sheet of a pile of papers on her desk.
   She said: "We serve lunch to anywhere from one to three hundred homeless men and women, four days a week." I waited for more, but she held off, the pencil moving in small circles on

the paper. She wore bold pink nail polish.

"As you can imagine, dealing with those kinds of numbers — and they are by no means always the same people either; far from it — we don't get to know them all. You say this person plays a flute?"

"Yes. Her name is Emily LeMoine. She lives in Grand Central Station but has been missing for a while. Just a day, really. I want to find her."

The woman put a hand to her mouth and waited. I thought she was thinking. Slowly her face changed, her lips drew in, and she sneezed three times, the tiniest, most contained, bird-like sneezes I'd ever heard.

"Bless you."

"Thank you. Allergies." She drew a pink tissue from a small square ceramic box and carefully touched her lips, then her nostrils. "I can't really help you. But you might come tomorrow at noontime. Maybe your — this woman will be here."

I nodded. "Does this church have stained glass?"

She studied me silently.

"It's relevant. Long story. She . . . Emily would more likely be in a place with stained glass. In fact, I'm looking for a place with ten stained-glass windows."

"We don't have any."

"Anyplace on the block, or near here, have stained glass?"

"The First Baptist Church on Seventy-ninth and Broadway. They have wonderful stained glass. But ten . . . ." She laughed. "No, unless you count Townhouse Row."

"What's that?"

"Townhouse Row?" She stood up. She was very petite, compact, but exuded a strange physicality, as if she could, if she wished, jump right over me from a standing start. "Along on Eightieth, just past West End, north side of the street. Go have a look. It's worth it. Architecturally. As long as you've come this far."

She herded me toward the door. "As I said, go look at it. It's quite historical. There's a sign there, designated city landmark, telling all about it. And come back tomorrow to check for your friend." I thanked her and was walking out the door when I turned.

"Oh," I said. "At least let me leave my card, on the chance that you might spot her, and perhaps you'll call me." I had my wallet out. "She's five seven, forty-two, looks older, knit cap, worn-out cloth coat. Emily LeMoine. And she's not well." I wanted to say the word, that ugly hissing label, had to try twice before it came out. "She's schizophrenic." I held my card to her and she took it. "Pleased to meet you, Mr. Transit," she said. Then, in an odd, breathless voice: "I'm Barbara." And she shut the door.

I drifted the few steps to West End. It was nearly dark now, and the wind was whipping through the street. I zipped my jacket. I felt vaguely drugged, as if being in that woman's presence had dulled my brain. From somewhere — must have been an apartment — came a high-pitched scream, a laugh, music: a blaring saxophone, a drum, cymbals, then nothing. A black four-by-four with oversized wheels, big chrome bumpers, and tinted glass flew by up West End. As it passed me, a head emerged from the passenger window, a man in a brown cap, his teeth amazingly white and somehow too long. He pointed at the sky, and as the truck thundered past, emitted a long, raspy howl.

I crossed West End and at the corner continued on, scanning the high, remote, dark facades of the buildings. Hoping to find what? Some mysterious townhouses with illusive windows behind which may or may not lurk a person to whom, at this wrecked stage of her life, I was drawn more compellingly and hungrily than when she was young and talented and beautiful.

Twelve

*T*he stained-glass windows were above the doorways of adjoining brownstones; identical Gothic arches with dark, irregular leaded-glass sections; heraldic turquoise shields in the centers and clear teardrop decorative insets. Embedded in the shields, the numerals of the building's addresses, 309 to 319 inclusive.

Was Emily in one of these houses? To see them better, I crossed the street, stood on the far curb, looking back. Number 309 had a brass lion's head with a door-knocker ring through its mouth. Number 311 had two-foot-high fleurs-de-lis carved into its facade near the corner. Number 313 had a door-high wrought-iron protective grille, 315 an ornate carved oak door with a small four-paneled window, 317 a large jutting second-floor bay window, set above which were more panels of stained glass. Dim light came from behind these. Number 319 was a four-story building with heavy wrought-iron bars enclosing dark ground-floor windows.

. . . pass under a white trumpet to stained glass times ten, and find her where love has pitched his mansion.

What now? Cross and start ringing doorbells? I stepped into the street to cross. A car horn blared and I jumped back. The same black four-by-four shot past me, horn blasting. I looked to see that nothing else was coming from Riverside Drive. Nothing. Past it, the park. Strange — among the dark shapes of leafless trees, an illuminated patch of white. Something in my mind ignited, a meaning of some kind, purely intuitive. I went down Eightieth, crossed Riverside to stand behind a three-foot wall. In the distance were lights, movement: traffic on the West Side Highway. But the white shape, well this side of the highway, kept my attention. Yeats! Your little joke. The rhyme, never ignore the rhyme!

> A woman can be proud and stiff
> When on love intent;
> But Love has pitched his mansion in
> The place of excrement.

The patch of white was a tent, on high ground, sixty yards into the park, half under the low bare branches of a tree. She could be there! It would make exquisite sense. The mansion *is* a tent. Not just a quirk of rhyme either, but Yeats' meaning: the low and the high in one place. Dared I believe this? I scrambled up onto the wall. A short drop to the ground. I stepped down onto something soft, which moved. I jumped sideways.

A shape like a log, bent in the middle, moving.

"Who're you, man?" A sharp, cramped voice from the shadowy form: a man in a sleeping bag.

"You a cop?"

"No."

"Then get the fuck away from me."

I did that, tripping backward. Most of me landed on hard ground, except for my head, which plumped into something soft.

I jerked free and stood up. Another sleeping form moved, emitting a snore. My eyes adjusted to the dark. All around me were people. Most in sleeping bags or under blankets. Some sitting up, propped against the wall I'd just come over.

I squinted in the direction of the tent and carefully picked my way through the patch of recumbent bodies. Then I was on a sidewalk, and ahead was an open area of grass, sloping up toward the trees where the tent was.

Fifty feet from the tent I heard the slapping of rubber soles on concrete. Through the trees dark figures ran north. Ahead of them came a high, fluttery cry, part laugh, part warning. It descended an octave and moved toward me, into the trees just past the tent, then choked itself off as a strained chuckle. An animal? A bird? Oh, that would be perfect, my special tormenting birds, come to meet me here! A trail of goose bumps rose in a tight ridge from the base of my spine to the nape of my neck.

I heard three breathy syllables: "Goddamn it," and then again, "Goddamn it," and realized it was me, and I broke into a run and then was at the tent — a long, narrow length of lightweight nylon supported at each end by a pole. The end facing me had a flap, and I threw it back and ducked down to see inside.

What happened next was very quick, taking maybe four seconds. I saw an upright wall of fur — no, matted hair — and for an awful first second I really thought I was looking at a huge monkey, its shoulders as hairy as its chest, its stomach expanding like a bellows. Between me and it was a smaller, darker form.

"Fuck," the thing spat, and I looked up to where it spoke from, and it was a human face, Caucasian, bearded, lips back, teeth uneven and dark. Frozen, I followed the line of his body back to his waist and below and saw he was attached to something there, which made raised, thick ridges around his hips. The near part of the smaller form moved sideways, and I was looking at a second face, this one upside down. She was young and female. The raised ridges were her legs. She had him in a strong grip, his dark pubic area welded to hers. As I stared, his right arm came up. I knew why, and I jumped backward, tripped and went down onto cold turf away from the tent, hitting my head on a rock.

I wanted to scramble up but I couldn't make my limbs move, and then the tent flap exploded outward and I saw naked thighs, belly, chest, shoulders, face, and he was right down on me, straddling me. Something was very different about his face now; a bulky metallic object where his mouth should have been. His hands found my wrists and pinned them, and he bent toward me. Only then did I see it: in his teeth, its black handle protruding past his right cheek like a waxed mustachio, its blade pushing his lips into a wide, manic smile, was a hunting knife.

His eyes were wide and blue. He was very strong. His face came down and down until it was five inches from mine, and he spoke around the knife.

"You come here to die?"

"No." My voice was high and strained.

"Maybe you gonna, though."

"It was a mistake."

"Got *that* fuckin' right."

"I'm looking for someone. Thought she was in there. No harm meant."

He released my left wrist, brought his hand up, gripped the knife handle, removed it from his mouth. The stainless-steel blade clicked against an upper incisor.

"You just open the door to someone's house? Huh? This is my house here. So maybe I just cut you somewhere as a lesson. Let you live but make you think."

I wasn't afraid, which surprised me: some other, more primal feeling had kicked in. On its own, my free hand extended back toward my head. I wanted the rock my head had hit. There was no question: he may cut me, but he'll pay. If it's my dying act, I'll bloody him. But in that instant he pushed up and back, and was standing over me, his penis half swollen, hanging strangely sideways, nearly across his thigh, his scrotum hidden in a deep bush of hair.

"Lucky for you I ain't the vicious type," he said. "Come in a man's home at night, anyone else would kill your ass."

My head was getting light, I wanted to get up but was afraid to; I was sure my knees would buckle. I risked it, and stood.

"I'm looking for someone."

"Tough shit."

"Woman, Emily, plays the flute."

"Why do you want her?"

"I'm going to help her."

"Help her what?"

I had no answer. Felt I might vomit; shock and fear were rushing up into me. I heard his words as if they came from far off:

"Get your butt outa here. Fuckin' do-gooder. Nobody needs your help. I could still cut your ass."

I was going back down the hill, staggering again. I stayed parallel to the highway, unwilling to be near the wall. Seventy-ninth Street was ahead; I could see lights there. The hill was exposed and the wind was raw, very cold, and suddenly my face was wet, the cold making my eyes water. Or something else was: the hard, pointed shard of defeat I felt forming in my gut. I felt utterly weak, not physically, but as a man, unable to carry through this one crucial thing — and yes, I probably was crying with rage at my insufficiency, my total failure. Which is when the smell came to me, both repellent and remarkable. I sniffed the air, trying to pinpoint wind direction. And when I knew I had it, the thought was: this is either suicide or deliverance. Fine; either is preferable to what I feel now.

The source of the smell was a quick four or five strides, along a wide walkway, past a thick tangle of bushes. I came to a high arched tunnel, made of blocks of cut stone, under the ramp connecting Seventy-ninth Street to the highway.

It was there, all right, emanating from the tunnel: the smell of human feces.

I went in slowly. The tunnel extended for perhaps twenty feet, and the arch on the far side was brightly lit. No one was in the tunnel, but people had been — it had become a latrine for a whole tribe. I was through it quickly. On the far side was a steep bank rising thirty feet to the right, with three leafless bushes and, higher up, a couple of leafless trees. On the left was open lawn and, sixty feet beyond that, four tall, powerful streetlights, which illuminated the area well, except for a small plot on the low part of the bank just beside the tunnel exit, where a deep shadow crossed the swale.

Just there, nearly out of view, was a shape. The light had temporarily contracted my pupils, and I waited for them to dilate, and then I saw that the shape was a cloth lean-to tucked against the bank. It was no more than a large faded blue sheet supported at the near end by a pole and anchored to the ground behind.

I squatted three feet from it and saw that the sheet was thin, insubstantial. Even as I looked at it, the wind shook it hard, causing an unsecured tail of it to flap like a sail.

"Emily?"

Something inside moved, and a voice came, thin as the fabric. "I'm cold."

I moved closer, face to the opening.

"Emily? It's Jack."

Nothing.

I reached for the flapping end of the sheet.

"Emily, are you in there?"

The voice said: "Who is it?"

"Jack."

A pause. "You have word from Daddy?"

I flung the cotton back. She was there, sitting, eyes like embers ready to go out, lips of a ghost, skin wildly luminescent in the light, and, most awful, most awful, her head, which had been covered with a knit cap in Grand Central, bare now, showing her hair, shorn close, a patchy stubble. Emily held a cotton wrap — a small sheet — tightly around her; she was shivering under it.

"Emily!"

The lips parted and the head went back. "Not till I get dressed."

Part of her sheet fell away, exposing a shoulder and an expanse of ribcage. She was naked.

"Where are your clothes?"

"They stole them again."

I had my jacket off, tried to get it around her shoulders. She backed up, deeper into her hiding place. I moved toward her.

"Jack, no. I'm embarrassed."

But I was into the tent now myself, forcing the jacket around her. She was freezing cold. She tried to back away further, but there was no room. She fought weakly, stopped, and I got her covered. A strange interval passed, five seconds. Both of us motionless, a crouching tableau frozen in time. Then she exhaled, shook her head as if at some private thought, and slowly, with what I swear was humor at the edges of her mouth, looked me full in the face, bent toward me, worked her arms around my waist, rested on my shoulder as lightly as a leaf, and embraced me.

Thirteen

She had no shoes, so I carried her out of the park. The sheet was still on her, like an untailored skirt, and I'd zipped my jacket around her. She was quiet as I carried her.

"Where's your flute?"

"Under the horse's flank."

"What horse?"

"The only one."

"In other words, you don't have it?"

"It's never something you *have*. You borrow it, lease it, enter it, swim up it, break apart and come out the stops, you're a hundred notes, your body is wind. Where are we going?"

"To get you warm and fed."

"Food is bad, contaminated. Better I should feed on myself, digest my own stomach, no problem, my flesh is pure."

"When did you eat last?"

"In the fourth century, I mean fourth stage of my life, I mean in the fourth quadrant, four-four time, number four train. The number four is a soldier saluting. Three is a human ear, two is a swan swimming, one is a steel beam seen in cross section."

I was carrying her up the Seventy-ninth Street hill from Riverside Drive to West End.

"Are you hungry?"

"No."

At West End I put her down, kicked my shoes off, unrolled my socks, and handed them to her.

"Put these on," I said.

"Not my style, too bulky."

"Put them on anyway." I slipped my feet back into my shoes.

She sat down on the sidewalk and put one sock on, stared at the other one. "This one is alive; wool shorn from a live sheep. This sock has feeling, like my foot. So a life meets a life. Will they get along? Do they see eye-to-eye? Who will be the dominant party — the sock or the foot? Who the more dependent? These questions can haunt a person."

I spotted a cab two blocks south. Stepped into the street, raised my arm. The cabbie approached, I opened the door, we got in. I gave the cabbie my address, and we moved into traffic.

"Where is that?" asked Emily.

"Just a few blocks."

"No, I mean what is there? Why are we going there?"

"It's my apartment."

Emily opened her door and started out. I grabbed her waist, hauled her back toward me. "Fuck," exclaimed the cabbie, and he put on the brakes. I fell forward and banged the side of my head on the plexiglass partition behind the driver. Emily jumped out of the cab.

I scrambled over the seat and chased her. She was running along the middle of the avenue, my socks flopping. I caught her, pulled her between two parked cars to the sidewalk.

"Who shot you?" she asked.

My head was bleeding from where I'd banged it. I touched it with my fingers.

The cabbie had stopped and backed up. "You all right?" he asked.

I said to Emily, "You going to get back in that cab?"

She shook her head.

"We're staying here," I told the cabbie.

"Well, that's a buck and a half."

"Give me a fucking break!"

He shrugged, moved slowly off. I turned to Emily. "Why'd you do that, for Christ sake?"

"Where you live is a dark place of mourning, a place for men and women in suits. Bright colors and recorded music. Furniture, windows, carpets, refrigerator. I won't go there. Red isn't your color."

She reached toward my head, but I pulled back, yanked a handkerchief from my back pocket, applied it to my scalp.

"Come on." I hurried her along, over Eightieth, to the church. I led her up the stairs and rang the bell. A distant door opening, a footfall, then a voice:

"Who is it?"

"Barbara? It's me, Jack Transit, from just before. The stained-glass windows? I need your help."

A pause, then a click in the door lock, and the door swung in.

Barbara stood looking at me. "What happened?" she asked, alarmed.

"I found her — Emily."

"But your head?"

"Nothing. Can you help us?"

"Well, come in. And here." She took the handkerchief from my hand and put it to my skull. "Hold it and press down," she said.

Emily said: "He may have been shot, but I've been misplaced."

"You were shot?" asked Barbara.

"No. I bumped my head. It's only a cut." Barbara led us into the foyer.

"They all say that," said Emily. "They learn it from the movies. It's not real-life dialogue, not real-life speech. It's fabulated. Fabricated. My, this is a nice church. I haven't been here. Look at how clean. Do you use Lysol?"

Barbara took us to her office and snapped a light on.

"I was literally on my way out. Would have been gone in thirty seconds."

"An eternity," said Emily. "Conception happens in less than a second, once sperm joins egg. Death happens more slowly, unless someone straps dynamite to your head and detonates it. Which happened to me twice."

Under the light in her office, Barbara assessed us. "You need clothes," she said to Emily. "I have a closetful to choose from. Jack, you need that cut cleaned and bandaged. I hope you don't need stitches. I'll take Emily inside for the clothes and you hold that hankie to your head till I come back."

She led Emily out, and I heard a door open off another part of the foyer, then close. I sat at her desk holding the wet handkerchief to my head. After a few moments, Barbara and Emily returned. Emily had on sweatpants, running shoes, and a bulky tan sweatshirt. "Quick, how many of me can dance on the head of a pin?"

I didn't get it, but then I saw, on the front of her sweatshirt, in bold green letters, the word ANGEL.

"Clever."

"Best I can do in these circumcisions."

"You mean circumstances."

"No, because you're sitting."

I looked at Barbara and raised my shoulders.

"Don't shrug me off," said Emily. "Circumstance, from the Latin *circumstantia*, which breaks into *circus* — literally a circle — and *stantia* — to stand. Circumstance: to stand around. Circumstantial then is that which depends on circumstances, pertinent but not essential. Facts or testimony you would expect from people not gathered for serious intent, but just standing around."

"Sorry I asked," I said, half joking, and a second later regretted it. Emily reacted as if she'd been hit. Her hands flew to her face, she ducked back, against the wall, and began to whimper.

Barbara went to her. "Did he hurt you?" she asked.

Emily nodded.

"People can hurt us when they don't mean to," said Barbara. "Would it help if he said he was sorry?"

Emily stared at me with such intensity I took a step back. It was the first time that she'd looked square into my eyes. She said, in a quiet, distant voice: "You are my husband. Love means never saying . . . love means . . . love means never . . . le vrai amour ne se change. Le vrai amour ne se change. J'aime mon mari toujours. J'ai donné mon coeur . . . I gave you my heart in New Orleans. You held my hand and walked me along Rue Helene, then we took the streetcar out past the Garden District, and the sun stood still, then passed overhead, smiled at us, and went down. And you walked me back by way of Rue Pierre Laffite to Jackson Square, and we had coffee. And your eyes were bluer than a robin's egg. I gave you my soul in San Francisco. You walked me along Fisherman's Wharf and through the Haight, and up Alameda Street, where you wrote poetry. Don't think I'll forget that; je me souviens. You were strong as life itself, and my hand was a fetus in the warm belly of your own. But Jack, mon mari, l'amour de ma vie, I never saw you in New York. New York is where we come to die."

I turned my face away. Something was pressing rhythmically against my upper lip: it was my own thumbnail.

After a moment, Barbara said softly: "Emily, why don't you sit there while I have a look at Jack's head." Emily perched on a chair and smiled. Barbara inspected my cut, took a bottle of hydrogen peroxide and a cotton ball from a cabinet, wet the cotton with the disinfectant, and touched it to the wound.

"You can't really put a bandage on it," she said. "Not unless you have it shaved first. But the bleeding's stopped. It's not that bad."

"Can we talk in private?" I asked.

"Okay."

She motioned me out of her office and into the foyer. Emily was perched on her chair, looking content. We left the door half closed, and moved ten feet across the foyer.

"I want her hospitalized. How do I do it?"

"Is she on drugs?"

"I don't know."

"You can take her to an emergency room. Bellevue. It's a quick fix. They'll put her in a bed, diagnose her condition, administer drugs if necessary. But they'll want to discharge her after that."

"I want long-term care."

"Then you're talking a private hospital."

"Do you know a good one?"

"Better to go through a psychiatrist. They've got clout in these places. And you better have money. Six months in a place like that can run fifty thousand dollars, a hundred . . . ."

"I can handle that. Meanwhile, is there a place she can stay tonight?"

Barbara shrugged. "Won't she go home with you?"

"No."

"She's best off with you until you can get her hospitalized."

"I have no experience. I'm not a doctor. I don't have those skills."

"Is there anyone else?"

"Yes. Can I use your phone?"

"Sure."

I went back into her office. Emily was still on the chair. She held her hands palms-up, fingers spread. She was counting. I picked up the phone and dialed: Six, six, one, eight, eight, zero, zero.

One ring, then a blast of sound — voices, laughter, rock music. A voice: "Tallulah Bankhead speaking. Who's this?"

"Is this Star Four?"

"Yes, and Happy Halloween!"

"Is Minerva there?" The noise was very loud. "I want Minerva. It's an emergency. About her mother."

I heard the phone at the other end drop on something hard, then a long loud moment, then: "Who's this?"

"Minerva? It's Jack again. I've found Emily. In Riverside Park."

"I can hardly hear you."

I said it again.

"I don't believe that."

"That's where she was. I need someplace to take her."

"Let me talk to her."

I cupped the receiver. "Emily, it's Minerva. She wants to talk to you."

Emily looked at the phone, at me. "I can't intrude on her, on her space, her life."

"She wants to talk to you."

I extended the receiver to Emily; she promptly sat on her hands. So I put it back to my ear.

"She won't talk to you."

"What the hell?" She was shouting over the line to make herself heard. "Tell her she has to go back to square one. Tell her I said so."

"What's that?"

"She knows."

"Tell me."

"Grand Central."

"No," I said. "I'm not in favor of that."

"Since when do you get a vote?"

"Since I saved her life twenty minutes ago, goddamn it."

"You did not!"

"She was freezing in that park. Naked except for a sheet, get it? She'd have damn well been frozen by morning."

Another long moment. She said something I couldn't hear.

"You have to speak up."

"Just get her back downtown, to the station."

Brainstorm! Came to me in a flash. "On one condition."

"Which is?"

"Meet me. Spend an hour with me. Anywhere you say."

A pause. She was thinking.

"You don't fucking give up, do you?"

"Never."

"Damn you!"

"Yeah, right."

She said something, but was drowned out by the noise. When

she spoke again her voice had changed. I wanted to think it had softened.

"Why is it so important to see me?"

"I'll explain that face-to-face. Name the place."

"I want her back in square one. So I'll meet you there."

"Grand Central, half an hour. At the information booth."

Another pause. "Minerva? Deal?"

"Okay."

"You'll be there?"

"I said I would."

"Thank you."

I gently hung the phone up, as if it were a living thing that needed care. I thanked Barbara, told her I'd call to let her know how things came out and try, somehow, to return the clothes. I hustled Emily down the church steps, out onto the street, and over to Broadway. It was alive with people in costumes. I hailed a cab, gave the cabbie our destination, reached across Emily and locked her door.

Fourteen

"This is great," I said to her. "This is great."
"Not really; the shocks are shot."
"Not the cab; what we're doing."
"What are we doing?"
Better dance around that one, I thought. Don't want her jumping out of any more cabs.
"Can you tell me why you left square one?"
"When he's there, I stay there. When he takes flight I have to fly with him."
"Pegasus."
Silence.
"So Pegasus left the station, and you followed him?"
Silence.
"Minerva didn't know. Does she usually know when you go somewhere?'
"Not if he tells me not to tell her."
"Pegasus told you not to tell her?"
She nodded.
"Did anyone know?"
"One who knows everything."
"The oracle?"

She grinned. "You know her?"
"No. But I'd like to. What's she like?"
"She's short."
"How does she know everything?"
Silence.
"Emily?"

She pursed her lips. In her lap her fingers worked nervously. So I eased up. We passed the Ansonia, and hit heavy traffic at Seventy-second Street.

"Emily," I said, "listen — is this the way you want to live?"
"In sweatpants?"
"No, here in New York, where it's cold —"
"If I have my music I'll be content, do a tour. St. Louis, Minneapolis, Houston, Santa Fe. Points south. Miami, Bermuda, Mexico City. They love me in Mexico City. I did a season there when Juan Milagro was conductor. He and his wife — what was her name? Anglo . . . Irene? Cynthia! Yes, she and I were great friends; we went shopping together. I like touring, and they miss me out there. Oh, and Taos. They have a fine new orchestra. I could be hot in Taos. I may go there in the spring."

Her hand was on the seat, and I slowly, experimentally, covered it with my own. It was cold. When she didn't pull it back, I enclosed it.

"What repertoire will you play?"
"I'd want to do Mozart, and Vivaldi, of course. I'd have to work up to the Bach. And I might play some Albinoni, some Campra, some Corelli this season. But forget that. I can't tour, not now, not like this. Not till Pegasus comes down to me."

I let that sit for just a second.
"Tell me more about him."
"He's my daddy, my everything. Daddy's taken on his body, his feathers, his skin, his sweat, his face, his man's great rod and swinging marbles. He is my sternest taskmaster. Only if I play perfectly will he come down to me, be with me. Yesterday I played nearly perfectly, within a pause of perfect, so he sent you."

"You're right. He sent me — do you know why?"

"To tell me about him! Prepare the way for him, for my reunion with him!"

Her eyes were wide like a child's.

"Yes, that's right."

"Start telling me, then. How is he? My daddy. How is he?"

"The time isn't right to do that now."

"When? Time's ticking on, and I have to hear his words, hear his instructions. He likes to come to me in the night. My daddy likes that. Do you know how it works? Our game? Our words?"

I didn't answer.

"Well, he announces himself. He comes to my door and knocks three times. I wait a moment then say: `Oui?´ And he says: `Petite, tu es prêt?´ Small one, you're ready? And I ask, in French of course, `But who are you?´ And he says . . . what do you think he says?"

Emily clapped her hands. "He says, `C'est moi, votre cheval!´" She laughed gleefully, fully. "Isn't it wonderful? It's me, your stallion! And I open the door and he gets into bed with me . . . and he . . . and we have secrets. You want to know our secrets? He touches me. Down there he touches me, makes me touch him, says only I can make him a stallion, a cheval rampant."

The cab lurched sideways. I took hold of the strap on the partition behind the cabbie's head just as Emily was thrown into me. She grabbed my knee.

"Are you going to touch me there?"

"No!"

"You can touch me there."

"No, no, Emily. No one must touch you there."

"You used to touch me there, and I liked it, even though you weren't Daddy."

And I knocked on the partition. "Driver, can you please slow down?" He did, and I sat back, wanting and not wanting to digest what I'd heard, in limbo between ignorance and knowledge. Emily leaned her head against my shoulder and seemed content, and we rode that way. We came to Columbus Circle, Central Park dark and dense to our left, and we took the spur to the right, past a small village of cardboard boxes and refuse in front of the abandoned Coliseum, where small fires burned and ragged people knelt before them, rituals beyond imagining.

At the streetlight where Broadway angles south, a procession of witches crossed ahead of us, stopping traffic, and a court jester followed them, playing a huge drum. Behind him was a prince with a gold cape and a gold crown.

I closed my eyes against it. Of course, I'd never known Thomas LeMoine, Emily's father; only seen pictures of him. He came from old money, was an amateur musician, a trumpeter who sat in on New Orleans jam sessions; his passion was breeding horses, and he'd died when Emily was young, killed in a riding accident.

Emily was very still beside me. "Your father. I'm trying to remember what he looked like."

She didn't answer. I thought she was asleep.

"Emily?"

"Yes, Daddy."

"I keep seeing a fence. He's standing by a fence. Remember?"

"Of course."

"And something's behind him. What was it?"

"Nothing."

"No, there's something behind him. But what?"

"Nothing. Nothing there."

***

Grand Central was more crowded than I expected. I saw Minerva right away, before we descended the stairs to the concourse. She was at the near side of the information booth. She wore an open black leather jacket, a black sweater, a well-worn jeans, and had a small bag over her shoulder.

I guided Emily down the stairs. Minerva saw us and came over. She said to Emily: "You tell. Did he save your life?"

"Yes."

Minerva took a breath. "Okay. Why did you go to wherever? Riverside Park. That's not part of our geography."

"I'm sorry."

Minerva looked at me. It was as though the lighting changed suddenly; became brighter. I was lost in her eyes, gray with flecks of green; wide, burning with intensity. Her wide mouth was disdainful. Again I had the uncanny impression that she looked down at me, though we were the same height.

"So why'd you do it?" she asked me. It was aggressive and arrogant, and I replied in kind: "You're going to make me defend saving her life?"

Her expression did not change, except to blend mild disgust into what was already there. Then she put a hand on Emily's arm and began moving away.

"Where are you going?"

"Down where she'll be safe."

"Where?"

"To her food and her bed."

She started off again. I stepped toward her.

"You'll come back?"

She turned abruptly. "*I* keep promises."

They skirted the far side of the information booth and headed across the station floor. Emily was small beside Minerva, who held her firmly, to keep her upright. They disappeared down a side passage, and I went quickly across the station floor to the spot and looked up. There he was — Pegasus. The ceiling was dark with grime, the image of the flying horse faded, difficult to discern.

> Our wedding clothes in a pile on the rug, Pachelbel, later to be changed for Jim Morrison, plays on the record player, we're on the bed, naked, the tart

taste of wine and goat cheese fresh in our mouths. We kiss deeply, kiss again, her hair falls across my shoulders, I feel her shoulder blades under my palms. I pull her to me, feel her breasts against my chest. I am aroused. She pulls away. Hold on, she says.

She reaches to the side table for a small glass box, begins making a joint.

Let's be straight tonight, I say.

She shakes her head. Of all nights, I'd think you'd want me relaxed now.

I caress her side, back, belly. You feel relaxed.

The joint is rolled, and she lights it, inhales, offers it to me.

I hold it between my fingers.

I love you so much, I say. I want you to be happy.

Happy is just what I'm going to be.

I take a shallow toke, hand the joint back, and she inhales greedily.

We make love. She has fabulous physical energy, an acrobatic imagination, a fine, sinewy body, power to burn. Long, gorgeous legs, which I adore. It was true — when she relaxed, when she was stoned, she was a lover on fire.

Most of all I love her hands, fine long musician's fingers, tiny muscles all honed from her playing, and as she spreads herself above me that night she rests her hands on my chest and rides me with a perfect rhythm. I take one hand, then the other, and kiss each finger: the nail, the pad, the first knuckle, the second, the third. Finally, the palm.

Then we roll over and I'm on top and she's all fury and sweat, grinding against me. "See, I can do it, I can do it, I can do it."

As she nears her climax, her voice becomes younger and younger; a girl's, really: "Daddy, Daddy, ride me, ride me. Okay, Daddy?"

I stood, viewing the ceiling, letting my eyes travel along the expanse of constellations, then coming back again to Pegasus. Memory! I tried to force it and drew only a blank screen, so I let my mind float, hoping to catch the thing unawares. *A man, standing near a fence, something behind him.* Then I got a smell: Burnt marijuana. And a sound: A creaking floorboard. And a sight: White lace.

>Morning. I awaken, get up, leave her sleeping under the covers, move toward the bathroom, walk gingerly because our apartment's old wooden floor creaks. Pass our dresser. What's on it? An ashtray, in it a spent joint. Acrid, stale smell. What else? A doily of Irish lace, an incense holder, my wallet, and — the photo, in a narrow wood frame. Thomas LeMoine. He's tall, good-looking. Riding trousers, white shirt. He leans against a rail fence, and behind the fence. . . . a horse. Huge white stallion in three-quarter profile, head up, eyes on the picture-taker. He looms behind and above LeMoine. Flying from his neck a full white mane, lifting in a breeze. Lifting . . . giving the impression, if you wished to take it that way, that along the stallion's neck was a pair of feathery outspread wings.

I looked up again. White wings, white mane. My eyes watered from the strain to see and my neck cramped from the effort, but I stood looking for a long time. Then I walked to the far side of the station, near the ticket windows. Train announcements clicking into position on the large board above. Finally, from the far side of the station came Minerva, alone. In a moment we were face-to-face.

"Emily's safe?"
She nodded.
"Will she eat something?"

"Yes."

"So then you'll give me some time?"

"I said I would." And then — miracle — she smiled. It softened her, made her more girlish. I felt my heart do something strange: it swelled. She is my daughter, and she is smiling at me.

Fifteen

She said: "Hi, Jeb."

Someone stood at my side, but it took me a long moment to connect what she'd said with him. Starting at the feet: heavy leather boots, tight aged blue jeans, a studded leather belt, a black T-shirt with a faded Norton motorcycle logo, a short blue denim jacket, a red bandanna, long straight black hair, and an absolutely cherubic male face, brown eyes, pale smooth skin, a strong jawline along which grew a nearly invisible stubble of beard.

He was a boy. Could have been sixteen, or a young eighteen. Minerva put a hand on his shoulder, kissed him behind the ear. He kept his eyes on me. Arm around him, resting her head on his shoulder, Minerva went languid, then whispered something into his ear. All the while he looked at me. No introduction was forthcoming so I said to him: "Hello. I'm Jack," and put my hand out. He hesitated, then responded; we shook. His hand was smooth and cool. When he spoke it was in a high-pitched voice, so quiet I had to strain to hear: "I'm Jeb."

Minerva looked from him to me. "We live together."

My reactions came fast, like firecrackers going off in a string. In order: jealousy, betrayal, anger. They were all irrational and all trouble.

"I'm caught off balance," I said.

"By what?"

"I thought it would just be you and me."

"Well, think again."

Jeb shuffled a boot against the floor. "Like I'm here to make sure, you know, she feels safe. She's like . . . safe."

"I want that too," I said. "I want her to be safe."

"Cut the shit!" Minerva said. "What are we going to do?"

I took a breath. "I was going to suggest a restaurant."

Her answer was quick, rhetorical: "Who's hungry?"

"It doesn't have to be about eating. In a restaurant we can relax, talk. That's all."

I dreaded her final no. She didn't issue it.

After a moment, Jeb said: "Pizza?"

"We can do pizza," I said. "We can do that. Though if we want to talk, you know, sit somewhere, let's just make sure it's somewhere comfortable, that's all. Find the right place." I didn't wait for an answer. "I've got an idea. An Italian place, Angelo's, near here. Comfortable, quiet, we can relax there. Good pasta, or you can just have a salad. Or nothing."

Minerva made an unpleasant face, with a small shake of the head.

I took a risk: "But you keep promises." Her eyes narrowed, bore into mine, locked me into a contest. If I was going to lose her, it would be from strength, not weakness.

Finally she exhaled, and there was a disdainful chuckle behind it. "Lucky for you."

"This way." I led them to the west stairway, was on the stair before I looked back. They were following. We went out and across to Forty-fourth Street. I was on the building side, Jeb near the curb, with Minerva between us, a step behind. We walked in silence, crossed Madison, and came to Angelo's. I opened the brightly painted green door and let Minerva and Jeb in ahead of me. A narrow bar with an expensive mirror. Beyond, a long narrow room, pink and white walls, linen table-cloths. Subdued elegance. We were all underdressed, but I was known there.

The hostess greeted us. I gave her my jacket; Minerva and Jeb held onto theirs. The hostess showed us to a table toward the rear. We passed a table of four well-fed, silver-haired men, looking at a dessert trolley. Ours was a round table set for three. The hostess indicated a chair to Minerva, and she sat. Jeb took the chair to her left, and I sat to her right. Minerva removed her jacket and put it over the back of her chair. I became aware of her shoulders, which were wide, and her breasts, which were high and full.

"This is what pizza shops are like in midtown?" she said.

"No pizza here, I'm afraid."

"Nice plates."

They were huge bone-china ovals — more the size of serving dishes — with elaborate scenes: in the background an Italian hillside and an arbor with snaky vines and florid leaves, and dominating the center, a crescent of five bees in flight, descending to a rosebush that grew up the side of the arbor.

Vincent, the captain, approached. "Good evening, Mr. Transit."

"Good evening, Vincent. I'd like you to meet my daughter, Minerva LeMoine."

"Ah," he said, bowing. "Enchanted."

"And her friend Jeb."

Vincent nodded at Jeb, eyeing him with distaste. "We're interested in a late dinner, spur of the moment. Hope we're not too casual."

"Would you care for a drink to start?"

"A Coke," Minerva said, and Jeb ordered the same.

"And your usual, Mr. Transit?"

"Thank you."

He left. There was a silence. "I bring clients here," I explained.

"Where we live, people eat three-day-old bread and drink five-dollar-a-gallon rotgut."

"Which is where?"

"Part of town you don't get to. Avenue B and Second."

"No, I don't get there." A pause. "Well, I hope you decide to eat. The food here is good, and I'm buying."

"You think we don't have money?"

"I wasn't thinking that."

"Yes you were."

"Sorry. We'll split it then."

Her lips were thin with disapproval. Jeb leaned to her and whispered. She shrugged and said, "No." He whispered again. "We'll be back," she said, and they both stood abruptly. I stood, too, and watched them walk to the door.

Vincent came with our drinks. Two Cokes and a scotch on ice.

"I did not know you had a daughter, Mr. Transit."

"Yes, I do."

"She's visiting?"

"No. She lives here."

"She is extremely beautiful, if I might say." I may have smiled.

"Young people these days . . ."

"How do you mean?"

"Oh, the gentleman . . ."

I smiled, shrugged. He left. In five minutes Minerva came back into the restaurant, alone. She approached the table and sat. I could not read her face.

"Where's Jeb?"

"Bailed out."

"Why?"

"Not comfortable here."

"I'm sorry."

"Why? You didn't want him here."

"That's not true."

"You'd prefer it was the three of us?"

"You wanted him here and it was okay with me."

"He didn't want to eat here. So he'll pick me up in an hour."

"All right." I had Vincent clear one place and one Coke. We sipped our drinks.

"So I had quite a day today," I said.

She did not respond.

"I went to the oracle and she told me how to find Emily. I found her, in Riverside Park, in a tent, naked except for a sheet. So what would have happened to her if I hadn't found her?"

"I don't know."

"She would have frozen out there —"

"What I can tell you," she interrupted, "is why she went."

"Yes?"

"Because of you."

"I doubt that."

"You've upset her. She thinks you're here as a messenger from Pegasus. I've told her you're not. What did you tell her? Did you say you were a messenger?"

"She came up with that, not me. She was convinced that's who I was. I insisted a couple of times that I wasn't, and that upset her. I hadn't seen her in eighteen years. I had to do something to open her up, keep her talking."

"That was a mistake. She was set up to think Pegasus was coming — flying down to rescue her. But he didn't, did he? He stayed up there on the ceiling, just like always. This terrified her — it's his rejection all over again. So she ran away. Okay, so then you go save her. Fine. That just gets you back to even, as far as I'm concerned."

Having no reply, I let that sit. Frustration came and went.

"Pegasus," I finally said. "What does she think he is?"

"Her father, who fucked her up good, then died on her. Did what fathers are good at."

"And her problem. She's what? Schizophrenic?"

"Tidy term."

"How long has she been this way?"

"All my life."

"Who raised you? Not her?"

Her eyes darkened. "What's it matter? The only question now is, what are you going to do?"

"What do you want me to do?"

"Maybe leave us alone. Maybe leave her alone, and me alone." Amidst her bristling and hostility, I felt calm, sure of myself. Her "maybe" was a sweet word, and I relished it. The response in me was: *I want to be your father*. The absurdity of this was nearly comic. I saw in that instant exactly where I stood: boxed in, a captive of my life, fenced off from my past, helpless. She was in charge because I wanted from her much more than she did from me.

"Are you going to go on hating me?"

She took time to think. "I should."

"I hope you don't."

Her face was bowed. Her hands were on the table, on either side of her plate, her left hand palm-down, her right one on its side, her pinkie touching the base of the stemmed water glass.

She has Emily's hands! Yet there was a difference: on the finger pads of her right hand were pronounced calluses.

I was looking at those when something dropped straight down — a vertical tube of light. I followed it downward, and there, near the center of her plate, enclosing one of the small roses at the side of the Italian arbor, was a small dome of wetness. I looked up to find Minerva facing me, mouth slightly open, a second tear on her cheek. She stood, took her coat, headed toward the door. I went after her and near the bar caught Vincent's eye. I said: "Leave the table as is."

There was traffic on the street, pedestrians on the sidewalk. Minerva had turned right and, hands in her coat pockets, was walking quickly east, back toward Madison. I caught up with her. She kept walking. I fell in beside her. She stopped abruptly just past a drugstore, where a tall metal gate blocked an alley, or a service entrance. Her face flushed. She spat the words out.

"You left us. Her and me."

"I did not."

"Bullshit!"

"Emily left. She left me."

"Bullshit!"

"What has she said?"

"You left us for some bitch whore."

"What? No! Listen to me now. One day I came home and she had packed my things and she told me she hated me, never wanted to see me again. Why? Because of a choice I'd made: to quit writing poetry. To go into advertising. Emily was an artist. Into the utter purity of art. She saw my choice as a betrayal. We were living in the Village. From the day I left she would have nothing to do with me. I didn't know she was pregnant. She communicated only through a lawyer. I loved her. Till yesterday I didn't know you existed. How could I?

"She hated business, hated money. It was the late Sixties, early Seventies. We were like that then. What could I do? I went on with my life, until today. But if I'd known about you, you'd have had a father. I'd never have quit looking."

"Why should I believe you?"

"Why would I lie?"

"It's what men do!"

"Why would I be going to all this trouble, seeking you out, to lie to you?"

"Guilt. Or you want something. Me on your side."

"What side? There aren't sides."

"Like hell. There are always sides."

"Minerva," I said, "come back inside the restaurant with me, please. Eat with me. After that, if you never want to see me again, okay. But give me this hour with you."

She said: "If it turns out you're lying, I'll kill you."

I believed she meant it. "Fine. That's a deal. And if it turns out I'm not?"

She had no answer.

"Come on, a deal goes two ways. If it turns out I'm not lying, I get more time with you? Time past today?" She was silent, which I took for assent, and I led her back to Angelo's. Vincent had left the table alone, and so we sat down.

We looked over the menus in silence, then ordered.

"How did you grow up?" I asked after awhile.

"My aunt Rebecca raised me."

"Really? She was in San Francisco when Emily and I were married. She and her husband — Fred — saw us off when we came east to New York. We split up. I never saw her again. Where were you born?"

"New Orleans."

"So Emily went back south?"

She nodded. "She moved us to San Francisco when I was two. She was already sick, had to be hospitalized. Aunt Rebecca and Uncle Fred took over. Emily couldn't take care of me. So they did. Then Fred got transferred here, and we all came east when I was eight. Here, Emily was in hospitals on and off, lived with us, disappeared, came back, was in other hospitals, but would never stay."

"Why won't she stay in hospitals?"

She hesitated. "See, the problem . . . it's not, like, that Rebecca and Fred didn't have money, but they . . . it takes sort of a lot of money for a good hospital. They thought city hospitals were okay — good enough. That's bullshit. They were scary — zoos. I personally got her out of one. She was tied to a bed frame, no sheet, nothing. I was fifteen. So I'd go to Fred and be like, `What's money for?´ and he'd be, `We can't afford it.´ They like had themselves to look after. Thing is, it's okay 'cause Emily likes the street. Wants her freedom. I don't blame her. I don't ever want her back in a hospital, period."

We were silent a moment.

"Where are Rebecca and Fred now?"

"White Plains. We haven't talked in six months."

"Why?"

"I wouldn't finish school. School had nothing for me. I wouldn't live up there either."

"Why not?"

"White bread, country club values, the kids' minds already like totally enslaved. I wanted to be in the city, I was born for cities." She drank. "This is the kind of place they come to in the city, when they come. Never been downtown, never seen . . . ."

I nodded.

"They're like totally negative. Don't like Jeb, don't like where I live, my clothes, where I work. And they totally don't like what I'm doing with my music."

Funny: that last word didn't register right off, as if it were foreign and needed translating. "What music?"

"I play guitar in a band. Jeb writes and sings. He's a beautiful poet. We play really weird clubs."

Blockage rose in my throat and I swallowed to clear it. "What kind of music?"

"Alternative. Rebecca thinks I'm throwing away my training."

"What training?"

"In San Francisco, I spent two years at the music conservatory, started when I was seven, and here I was in the Mannes College of Music."

"I thought you dropped out of school . . . ."

"White Plains High School, where the only music was band music they needed for halftime at football games. Can you see me in a marching band? Anyway, I did about six years all told of classical guitar. I studied here with Sergio Palmatto — he was Segovia's best pupil. Palmatto takes about four students a year, and he took me, and I spent three years studying with him. I —"

"What?"

"Won awards. I have Vivaldi, Purcell, Praetorius — a good intermediate classical repertoire."

The blockage hadn't gone anywhere, and I knew everything it was telling me. That maybe in life you do sometimes get a second chance. And I was looking at mine.

I said weakly: "I didn't know you were a musician."

She cocked her head; again anger, a touch of disdain, and then a sort of calm reflectiveness.

"So that makes us even. I didn't know you were a poet."

"I'm not," I said.

Sixteen

*O*ur food arrived and we ate. I ordered Chianti. Vincent brought two glasses and she drank a little. Minerva had ordered scallops; she had a precise, studied way of choosing one, assessing it, raising it slowly, experimentally, to her mouth, chewing it with great interest, then, poker-faced, choosing the next one.
"Good?"
She nodded.
I wanted a show of more pleasure.
"You sure?"
Again the nod. I offered her a taste of my broiled tuna, which she accepted.
"Tell me about your world."
She wiped her mouth. "Club scene . . . downtown scene . . . music . . . ."
She talked about her New York — Alphabet City, Tompkins Square, clubs — and where she lived, a fifth-floor walk-up in the East Village. She said they had a neighbor, a onetime stockbroker who'd lost his job, left his family in Connecticut, was beginning a second life as a painter. He painted tiny canvases depicting paper currency in various stages of biodegradation. Rotting dough, he called it.

"Picture a painting maybe six inches square. An ugly, bloated black-and-green rectangle floating against a background that might be landfill, might be a wall, or just brown sky. The rectangle — is it flesh? Vegetable? A nightmare? What it looks like is something that's been in the refrigerator for a month. Just plain rot. You can almost smell it.

"Now one little section of this . . . thing — maybe a corner, maybe in the middle — is different. You have to look very close, even use a magnifying glass, and what you see is that it's a dollar bill. He has one, for example, that shows at the bottom, in the middle, the chin and coat of Alexander Hamilton, under that, `Ha,´ the first two letters of his name, and under that the `Do´ of `Dollars.´ So you know it's a ten. Another one just has a border and a lot of spidery lines at the corner, and the top of a `2´ and a `0.´ A twenty. Always, the one little area that isn't rotted is perfect. He wears jeweler's glasses and uses tiny brushes to paint the details. I asked him why his paintings were so small, and he said because his apartment is tiny. Jeb doesn't buy that: he says they're small because they're so ugly."

"Has he sold any?"

"No: he refuses to. Says it might lead to success, and it was success that ruined his life the first time around. `Why should I trade perfectly bad money for good?´ Isn't that funny?"

"It is."

I sipped my wine.

"Tell me about your work," she said.

I told her about my office, Carl, the new Mercedes account. And about other accounts — cereal, shampoo, an airline, a resort chain. I told her about Tom Blackwell, who knows everything about mythology.

"If it weren't for Tom, we wouldn't be sitting here."

"Why's that?"

"He steered me to the oracle."

She raised her eyebrows.

"You know her?"

She nodded.

I was excited. "Tell me about her."

"She comes and goes, been in Florida for a few weeks. How she gets there I don't know. Everyone Emily knows travels around, most of them just around the city. Emily sticks pretty much to Grand Central now, except — well, like today."

"The oracle — is she psychic?"

"Some people think so. I don't. She's got a great mind, real intuitive. Plus, she can get anyone to open up to her, tell her their innermost thoughts, what they want. People like come to her, confess things. She knows everything about everyone. Been on the streets for years. The word is she was once a teacher and a writer — yeah, wrote textbooks."

"Listen, if the oracle knew where Emily was the whole time . . . I mean, then what they put me through — the riddle and everything — was a charade. An elaborate scam."

"Not from their point of view."

"Yeah, well, meanwhile Emily was damn near freezing to death. With friends like that, she's lucky she's alive."

"She's a cat," said Minerva. "Has nine lives."

"I wonder."

"Look, on the street, you live on the edge, okay? It's just the way it is."

"Not really. No one wants to live that way."

"That's naive."

Her words irritated me. I should have let it drop. "It's not naive. These people should at least stick together."

She shook her head.

"You don't think so?"

"*Should* doesn't enter into it. They do what they do. It's never pretty."

"They would have let her die out there?"

She made an aggressive gesture of dismissal. "Life up here, with the suits, is all love and roses? I bet people get screwed good right in these places, over pretty plates and white wine, get fucked over, sold down the river, only it's done differently — different style, that's all. Huh? But hey, this is your life, right? Just so you know, it's another fucking planet. Be glad you have it. I have to decide what life *I* want, what life *I* can have. It's not going to be hers, thank you. But not yours either. So keep your judgments. They're like really stupid."

I wanted to be angry but rejected that. I wanted to be wise, but I knew I wasn't. I was blank. A traveler in a country so foreign that my ignorance was monumental and comical. A waiter came and cleared our plates.

* * *

We stood at the curb, Minerva looking east on Forty-seventh Street while I leaned against a mailbox, hands in my pockets.

"What time is it?" Minerva asked.

"Ten forty-five."

"And we got here about nine?"

"A little after."

"So he's late," she said.

The lights of the city were hard on my eyes. Somewhere toward Grand Central a symphony of car horns erupted, moved north, faded. She leaned against a pole that supported the restaurant canopy. Light from a streetlamp fell on half her face, making the skin appear translucent, illuminating one eye, hiding the other.

"I think you scare me," she said.

"How?"

"Because you're normal. I probably want to be like you."

"Your music, your playing . . . it's good?"

"Sure. I live for it."

"You make money?"

"We split like two hundred a gig. Four of us. Maybe a gig a week."

"That can't go too far."

"I make my living money at Star Four, tending bar."
"I see."
"Tips are real good. I can cover expenses and still save a hundred, maybe a hundred and a quarter, a week."
"Saving toward . . . ?"
"School."
"College?"
"Conservatory. Finish my training."
"The conservatory . . . ."
"In San Francisco. That's what I want."
"Why out there, instead of here?"
"I started there, I want to finish there. Faculty's excellent. And Jeb hates it here. Says he can't be a poet here. He's given me till spring, says he has to split."

I said with forced casualness: "So off you go."

"Not that easy. Emily wouldn't last a week without me. And she won't leave New York. Hardly ever leaves Grand Central. Has to always be playing there . . . ."

"So she's all that's keeping you here?"

Her answer was cut short by a roaring along the street. It rose in pitch and shattered the quiet. I turned to look toward Madison and there he came — Jeb, astride a motorcycle, a dark figure on a massive machine, moving toward us like an animal of prey. Minerva stepped away from me and waved; she was on her toes, her body straining toward him. I saw the long lines of her calves tighten and define themselves, her calves rise and harden, and through that musculature I saw desire, her yearning for him, toward him, away from me.

Jeb stopped at Minerva's side, extending a foot to support his and the bike's weight, and pulled off a shiny black helmet. His long hair was matted. Minerva went to him, ran a hand through his hair. "You're late."

She kissed him, he moved a hand around behind her neck, held her to him lightly, moved his hand up and through her hair. He stroked her, his face hidden from my view by her head. She leaned in, and everything was quiet except the throaty idle of the machine, and some other, subtler sound. I tracked it to them. It was a kind of groaning, but of pleasure.

Minerva swung a leg across Jeb's bike and mounted behind him.

"Look," I said, "about Emily. Maybe we should make a plan."

"What kind of plan?"

"Some way to help her. Some way for me to help."

"She doesn't go along with plans."

"But what's to keep her safe now? Why won't she run off again?"

"Nothing. She might."

"I want her somewhere safe."

"She won't go. And anyway, it would cost a shitload of money."

"I'm not worried about that."

Jeb cranked the handlebar accelerator, racing the motor. I was desperate. "Hold on."

I pulled out my wallet, extracted one of my business cards, and wrote my home address and phone number on the back of the card. I held it toward Minerva.

"So you can get to me. I have your number."

She eyed the card and for an awful moment I thought she was not going to take it; but she did, put it in her bag, then she settled back, putting her arms around Jeb's waist. I stood watching them and felt a gnawing incompleteness. I wanted so much from her, and was entitled to none of it.

Seventeen

I went home, slept for twelve hours. Arose, showered, shaved. Stared at myself in the mirror. An odd sense of being fractured — as if there were two reflections in the mirror. A Jack I knew and a stranger. I stared into my own eyes.

> A mirror, steamed over. Behind me, in the tub, Emily, showering. I wipe the mirror, revealing my face bearded with foamed soap. Damp hair to my shoulders. I apply safety razor to cheeks, chin, neck.
> Water stops, shower curtain pulled back. Tell me again, says Emily. You were brilliant. How brilliant? Beyond words; Carnegie Hall won't be the same.
> She steps out of the shower, towels off. You're not just saying that? Sure, just as the *Times* is just saying that. They did like me. Loved you. Her hands around my waist. We've arrived. You certainly have. And you with me.
> Coffee smell. Tiny kitchen table. Bagels, cream cheese, jam. Bagels, I say, never get these in San Francisco. I won't miss them. I drink coffee, she spoons jam onto a bagel. Emily. What? I got a job. Where? Ad agency.

The metallic *clunk* of her spoon striking the tabletop. You're a poet! You write poetry. I have to do more. There is nothing more. Our eyes lock. I want to go back home, she says. This can be home. Not mine. Give it a year; make our base here for a year; you'll be touring two-thirds of the time anyway. I want New York and this job for a year. Please. But that you would get a job without telling me; what is that? I was afraid to tell you, the way you get.

Our livingroom; both standing. I married a poet. You married a writer. Not a fucking salesman. Everyone's a salesman; think your playing isn't about selling? If people didn't buy it you couldn't play it. That is so twisted. You play for money; I want to write for money. I play for art; that's what we're about, not fucking commerce. Don't get holier than thou. Suddenly her face dark. She's shaking, whispers: Don't destroy your soul! Oh, come on. Think you can't? It's easy.

My soul is tied up with yours; ruin yours and you ruin mine!

What are you talking about?

***

I walked to work. At the office Irene sat at her desk. "Good morning."

"Morning."

"Now what?"

"Huh?"

"You look terrible again."

I went to the kitchenette for coffee, brought it back. Sat at my desk, sipping it. Looked through the written messages. All were business calls except the last one, which was from Pete, dated two-thirty P.M. the previous day and requesting a return call. I stacked the messages neatly in a pile, accessed my voice mail. Four messages there, three internal: from Tom and Michelle, asking that I get back to them. One from Gordon. Then the last one:

"Jack, it's Mary. I hate myself for it, but I'm thinking about you. That's all." My intercom rang; I picked up.

"Ten-thirty," said Irene. "They'll be starting in Carl's."

I put the handset down, thought, picked it up, and called Pete. His secretary put me through.

"Pete, it's Jack."

"Hey, buddy. Listen — wasn't I going to hear from you about dinner last night?"

"Yeah."

"What happened?"

I took him quickly through what had happened.

"Christ," he said finally. "How do you feel?"

"Numb."

"What are you going to do?"

"No clue."

"Well, look, we've got a squash game on the books for tonight. You up to it?"

"Fucked if I know."

"We can cancel."

"No, let's do it."

"Well, think about it, call me back."

"No," I said. "I want to."

"Okay," he said. "Seven o'clock."

I hung up, stood, left my office and headed for Carl's office. Underfoot the thick red carpeting of the corridor. This is a safe place. Here I know all the rules.

Carl sat at his desk, feet up, a cigar the size of a small cannon turning his lips lopsided. Gordon was on the couch, Charlie Wend and Dick Hopkins were in chairs.

"Jack," said Carl, half yelling, "come on in."

Dick came over to me. He was a tall, angular man with a long face and a lean frame. Dark hair slicked back, black Italian suit, gray turtleneck, expensive designer eyeglasses. He was vice-president for new business, and head of our L.A. office. "Hey, tiger!" He hugged me.

"Yowza."

"Like the man of the hour. The man who brought Mercedes to heel."

"You look good. I love that suit."

Dick fingered a lapel. "Giandelli; he's new. Forget Armani — this is it. New Age kind of Italian guy, as in Milan, consults his astrologer every morning, rides a bicycle when the Maserati's down. Love the guy."

"Very L.A."

"Whatever."

Charlie Wend had come over and shook my hand. Carl had hired him six months before to run our Chicago office; the report so far was mixed. Short, wiry guy, perpetual smile, a high forehead, small mouth. His forte was supposed to be transportation and media accounts.

"Look at the tan," I said.

"Is that a goddamn tan?" said Carl from where he sat. "We send a guy to Chicago, and does he come back with business? No, he comes back with a tan. Something's wrong."

"Nobody ever got a natural tan in Chicago," Gordon said. "Must be one of those tanning booths."

"No, man," said Charlie, "there's sun in Chicago. Spend a coupla days on a sailboat on Lake Michigan, you get a tan. No big mystery."

"What're you doing sailing around Lake Michigan," said Carl, "when you should be knocking on doors on Michigan Avenue?"

"On weekends? Knock on doors on Sunday? Talk to cleaning ladies?"

"Knock on goddamn doors at midnight, I don't care. Just get us business!"

"Jesus, you just landed the biggest plum of your lives, and you want more business?"

"I always want more business, fella." The edge in Carl's voice apparent to everyone.

Charlie and Dick went back to their chairs, and I joined Gordon on the couch.

Carl's feet were still on his desk and as he moved them the leather of his shoes squeaked expensively. "Okay, we got Troutbeck for the weekend, Jack is gonna organize things up there, get the creative brains rockin'. Bottom line is we gotta sell cars! There's gonna be price resistance, Japanese comin' at us with Lexus and Infinity, Swedes with Volvos and Saabs. I don't have to tell you. How we gonna sell this car? Two words: heritage and class. Lexus and Infiniti don't resonate, they don't have a hundred years of tradition behind them. Volvos are boring and Saabs are weird. And our hook, our sex appeal, is racing. It's a gut thing like we've said all along. Our focus groups show it, our research shows it, Jack sold it big time to Mercedes, which — lucky for us — just happens to be back in it big after thirty years."

"Thirty-*five* years," said Charlie. "Ever since a 300 SLR sliced a bunch of people in half on the front straight at Le Mans in 1955 —"

Carl interrupted. "Think I don't know that? Think I don't know history, racing, that shit? I eat and breathe it, goddamn it. Hey, who was driving that 300?" He looked from one to the other of us. "Anyone know that?"

I knew but I kept quiet.

Carl answered his own question. "The driver was Jacques Lefevre."

Charlie chuckled. "That's easy. Who nudged him off the track?"

Carl shot him a look. "That's easy too. American, Bill Catlin, driving a Corvette."

Charlie grinned. "Negative. It was a Healey."

"Corvette, goddamn it."

"It was a Healey, Carl. A Mark III with an aluminum body. Lefevre had passed him at the White House turn and Catlin didn't get far enough right, touched the Mercedes' rear fender, thing was going a hundred and fifty, knocked it over the wall and killed —"

Carl's face reddened; he dropped his feet to the floor. "Can it, Wend. I say it was a fuckin' Corvette. Go look it up if you have to be a wiseass. I pay you to give me this kind of shit?"

Charlie turned the color of chalk.

After the right amount of time, Gordon spoke:

"If we can get back to the advertising? Those days are long gone, another era, another generation. We're talkin' spots built around the new racer, the C291, print ads, the mystique of racing, very heartbeat, very visceral. That, by the way, is where all the other brands got squat, who ever raced a Volvo, you kidding me? BMW maybe, Jaquar maybe, and that's it. Right, Jack?"

I was questioning my sanity because of a thought I'd just had. I have no idea what my expression was. Possibly blank, possibly cartoon-animated. Carl was staring at me.

"Jack?"

"Listen, we're getting ahead of ourselves. This is what we'll sort out when we get away."

"Just batting ideas around," said Carl.

"No, I know, that's fine, I'm just saying we'll go at it full bore in Bucks County, structure the talk, structure the thinking, explore everything."

"Okay," said Carl. He was looking at me intently.

"We've got a lot of dynamics here. Lot of options," I said.

"What dynamics?"

"Possibilities."

Carl looked at Gordon. "What's he talking about?"

Gordon shrugged.

"It's nothing," I said. "Just a thought."

"So let's have it."

I exhaled. "A whole other way to sell this car."

Eyes clawed at me, ate around my edges.

"What other way?"

"Safety."

A silence, no saying how long.

"... the fuck? ..." said Carl.

Charlie laughed.

"We keep letting Volvo get the high ground on safety testing. Why?"

"Safety's boring," said Charlie.

"Not to a guy with a wife and two kids."

Carl said: "Volvos are fucking boring!"

Gordon said to no one and everyone: "I never thought I'd hear Jack the Ripper come on with a platform aimed at a guy with a wife and two kids." Then to me, a challenge with no trace of humor. "You gettin' old, pal?"

"Listen, racing will get interest, it's sexy, no question, maybe we soften them up with that. But people need more. The nineties are going to be conservative, you better believe it. People need a shitload of justification to part with sixty G's to buy a car when banks are failing and real estate is shaky, okay, and when they can get a couple of goddamn good machines for a whole lot less. Lexus is what? Forty at best? I see a campaign maybe with the sex of racing, but just as a door opener, then followed up with a lot of practicality, a lot of common sense, and safety is on top there."

When Carl spoke he spaced his words as if each one weighed a pound and they were a relief to put down: "You sold Mercedes on racing. They bought racing. They want a campaign on racing. They expect it."

"They want to sell cars," I said. "Let's sell what people are looking for. Nothing new in that."

"No!" said Carl. "For-fucking-get it."

There was a long silence in the midst of which Dick suddenly and rather violently yawned.

"Sorry," he said. "When's lunch?"

"Lunch," Carl said. "Christ, what time is it?"

"Eleven."

"So I didn't have breakfast," said Dick.

"You still doing granola," said Gordon, "and whatever the hell ... grape leaves?"

"I don't do grape leaves. I do sunflower seeds."

"Whatever."

"We gonna sit here discussing what Dick has for breakfast for Christ's sake?" asked Carl. "My creative heavy hitter has just suggested we sell a Mercedes like it's a Volvo and nobody has anything to say?"

In the room, silence. On Carl's face, dismay. In my mind, rebellion.

"Can't hurt looking at it from another angle," I said. "I'm telling you these are different times, that's all."

"Well why didn't you come to us with this before? Why now?"

"Good ideas come on their own schedule."

"Bullshit!"

Carl leaned back, took a deep inhale on his cigar, and we all watched intently as he sucked it in, held it, looked from one to the other of us, then slowly, elevated his chin, pursed his lips and out the smoke came in a thin, elegant line, forty-five degrees from parallel, traveled across his desk going up, shattered in moving air.

Charlie, out of absolutely nowhere, said: "So listen, Dick, you still doing crystals?"

"What do you think?"

"What do you mean, what do I think? Are you doing them?"

"Am I staying in touch with correct creative and spiritual power?" asked Dick. "The answer is yes. What are you doing to improve your life?"

Charlie was pleased to be talking. "Oh, listen to him. What am I doing to improve my life? I'm not buying fifteen-hundred-dollar suits some guy on a bicycle designed."

"That's because no one in Chicago knows the difference between a two-hundred-dollar suit and a fifteen-hundred-dollar suit. And I should know — I worked that cow town for twenty years."

"Would you listen to this? The man does crystals and eats grapevines for breakfast and he dumps on a city where you can at least tell the men from the women."

— 139 —

"Have I just gone insane?" said Carl. "Is that it? Because this meeting is as of now totally cockeyed."

"Maybe Jack's onto something," said Dick. "What's the hurt of looking at it?"

"I don't change paddles in midstream," said Carl. "Gordon, what do you say?"

"We have to deliver racing. It's what they bought. We fuck around we'll lose the account."

"I'll make a deal with you," I said. "I'll give you that campaign and a backup — safety, practicality, value for your dollar."

"But we don't need a backup."

"Indulge me, just this once."

Carl threw his hands wide, pointed at me. "Do I kill him or throw money at him?"

"You guys don't like the backup, we scrap it. You like it, we go to Mercedes with both. We present two campaigns, one your way, one mine, and see which one they prefer."

"You fucking serious?" shouted Gordon.

***

Outside Carl's office I caught up with Gordon. "Can we talk?" I led the way to my office. "You as upset as I think you are?"

Gordon paced my rug. "No one goes to a new client with that kind of surprise. Give 'em what they fucking want, what they bought. Jesus."

"What about the strategy behind the other idea. You hate it?"

Gordon stopped pacing. "I hate change, Transit."

"Yeah?"

"Yeah. And that's what I'm getting from you lately. Change. When everything's fine and we're in clover. It's irrational."

"We can always be better."

"Most change makes things worse. There's a lot riding on this creative. Everything, in fact. You fuck it up, it's my career too, my life." He started for the door. "You came on pretty strong."

"Yeah, I did. I'm sorry."

"Okay."
"I think we see things differently," I said.
"I think we do," he said.
"Still, let's stay friends."
"Long as you don't fuck up Mercedes, I'm your buddy."

Eighteen

*P*ete was in the locker room. He wore sweatpants and a light sweater and was sitting on a bench, tying his shoes. I dropped my workout bag, shook his hand. "Hey, buddy, sorry again about last night."

"No problem. Glad you want to play."

He stood, picked up his squash racquet.

"See you on the court."

"Right. Give me ten minutes to stretch."

As soon as I walked on the court and hit my first ball, I knew it was one of those days when things would not be in sync. I moved awkwardly in the warm-up, hitting balls harder than I wanted or not hard enough; every fourth or fifth shot missed the racquet's sweetspot. We played two games and I was late getting to balls, off balance once I was there. I lost 9 — 5, 9 — 3. We came off the court for water, and I was more winded than I should have been.

"You okay?" said Pete.

I nodded, thinking things would change in game three. But I was not clearing well and interfered with two of his shots, crowding him too close.

Pete won the third game, for the match, then we played two more, and nothing improved for me. My mind had disconnected from my body; I was numb. Coming off the court this time I threw my racquet down, picked up the towel, threw it down, sat in a chair, put a towel over my face. My head ached.

"Come on," said Pete. "Let's get a shower and something to drink." I pressed the towel to my face, eyes. "Jack?"

***

Showered, combed, dressed, Pete and I went upstairs to the members' lounge, settled into chairs, he with an orange juice, me with a seltzer on ice. I felt hollowed out, depleted, and my head ached.

"So, Minerva," Pete said. "What's she like?"

"Mature for eighteen, strong. She's a musician. Plays guitar, has classical training. Needs to go back to school to put the finish on her music. She'd go to San Francisco if she could. She has a boyfriend who wants her to, but I don't think she'll leave Emily.

"Thing with Emily — I learned things about her I never knew. Her father abused her . . . incest like at age five. He died when she was eight, in a riding accident, crushed under a horse. I never knew this, any of this, when we were married."

I sipped my drink. "Emily did a lot of drugs when I knew her — pot, hash, acid. Hell, it was nineteen sixty-eight, sixty-nine, seventy, seventy-one — people lived on chemicals. Then she got . . . different, critical of me. Angry all the time, hated it that I wanted to go into advertising. I shouldn't have let her drive me out. I should have stayed."

Pete put his glass on a table. "Listen. We had someone in my office, intern fresh out of college, really bright, attractive kid. Halfway into the summer, he broke up with his girlfriend on a Friday night, and his mother died two days later. Kid cracked, had to be hospitalized where he was forced to wear mittens twenty-four hours a day because he kept scratching, clawing his own face. Didn't talk for two weeks, finally did, said that he was an airport, planes were taking off from the top of his head, people were riding in tiny trains through his body to finally arrive in his mouth, behind his eyes and ears. At night they came out, little people, walked up his face to get to the planes. He had to scratch them, claw at them to keep them off his face.

"Deal is his father'd been a pilot, crashed a Piper Cub while the kid, aged six or seven, was waiting for him to land. Kid saw the crash, saw his dad pulled out of the wreckage of the plane."

"So what it means is if he hadn't broken off with his girlfriend the same weekend his mother died, would he have been okay?"

"Don't know."

"If Emily hadn't split with me — if I hadn't forced her to, just hadn't changed — would she be okay today?" I didn't give him a chance to answer. "I should have seen it coming, known her — what would happen."

"Do you *want* to feel guilty for the rest of your life?"

"Well what's the lesson of your story?"

"Human nature's a mystery. Not the father's fault, what happened to his son — hell, the father was killed. Not your fault what happened to Emily. She drove you out. Her demons got her."

I took another drink of seltzer. "You love someone for a while, then it goes away, but the part of you that loved lives on. I haven't loved since Emily. I reject women. I want to make it right with Emily, but how? Want to get close to Minerva. How? She doesn't need me. I had my moment, my twenty-four hours of fatherhood. The end."

Pete shook his head, a dark gesture, one I could have asked him to explain. I rubbed my temples.

"You okay?"

"Exhausted."

"Go home and sleep."

"What haunts me . . . is by trying to help Emily I'm being as selfish as when I left her. Doing it for me, to find me."

"Since when is finding yourself selfish?"

***

At home I lay on the couch, lights off, an ice pack on my head. Silence in the apartment, silence outside. Please, no more memories.

> Her veil. Flowing behind her, antique white lace, once her mother's and grandmother's, now hers. Cotton granny dress with paisley print, a headband of yellow daisies, wire-rimmed glasses. My shirt open to my chest, wide-lapeled suit with bellbottoms, my silver necklace and peace pendant dangling, hair in a ponytail.
> Musicians, friends, strangers follow in procession out of Golden Gate Park, into the Haight. Her veil blown back in the breeze; white, feathery, flowing behind her. Stopped at an intersection to dance, banners flying, people leaning from second-story windows, shouting, laughing, stoned. Someone hands Emily a flute; she plays "When You Come to San Francisco."
> We dance up Ashbury past Waller and Frederick, toward the house we share with assorted others. I take Emily's hand, we stand in the street, locked in an embrace. We did it. So call me Mrs. Transit. Mrs. Transit. She kisses me. Love me forever? Oh, yes. Music forever? Yes. Poetry forever? Yes. Daddy, kiss me.

I sat up. Sweating. Picked up the phone, dialed. Mary answered.
"It's me."
"Hi."

"Can you talk?"

"Okay," she said. "But before you start — I met someone."

"Fast work."

"Just a second date."

The headache a scalpel in my brain. "Who is he?"

"What's it matter?"

"This hurts me," I said. Silence. "I've been trying to think . . . listen. The difference between us — you know yourself, what you want. I . . . know I . . . what other people call love, what that is . . . I do have it for you. But not in a way you can use. It's tangled inside me. Because I don't know me. If I don't know me, I'll just hurt you — guaranteed. Not knowing me, I destroyed Emily."

"That's pretty harsh."

"Take my word for it."

"Okay." Silence.

"How . . . what's the trick of knowing who you are?"

"Knowing what you're not. Take what isn't you, cut it away. You're what's left."

"Spoken like a surgeon."

"Thank you."

"I'm not there yet. Can't fake it."

"Yeah." She sounded resigned. "You said you love me. How do you know that?"

"Thought of you with another guy kills me."

"Maybe we can work with that."

"Don't have a third date, please."

"That's a tough one."

"Can we discuss it over dinner?"

"I'm not free till next week," she said.

"Okay."

"What night?"

"Shit, we're in Bucks County next week. Brainstorming Mercedes."

"The week after." A frightening, terrible yearning caught hard in my throat. I had no words to put to it.

"You'll be in bed with him by then. Pregnant probably."
"That a joke?"
"No."

When she spoke it was matter-of-factly, and cruelly so: "Call me when you're ready."

***

In Bucks County we hammered out a lot of advertising. Premises for a TV campaign, copy platforms for print, graphic approaches for all media. Racing theme with its subsets: snobbish theme, unmatched-engineering theme, best-car-money-can-buy theme.

And the safety theme. No one there bullish on it but me. But I kept hammering on it, developing it, working up some print and television concepts around it, promoting it.

On the third day Michelle O'Malley took up my cause, began feeding me ideas of her own. Once, reaching across my arm to write a thought on my yellow pad, she balanced her right breast delicately on my forearm and let it rest there.

My suite was on the top floor of the conference center and most of the others were two floors below. That night, after a good dinner with excessive wine, a knock at my door roused me from semiconsciousness. It was two-thirty, and the wine still worked in my head. I stumbled to the door. "Who is it?"

"Michelle."

I opened the door. Her hair down. Beige silk blouse, dark slacks, black high-heeled shoes.

"Can I come in?"

The scent of her perfume hit me — enveloped me — so that I felt something loosening in me instantly, an unconscious guard coming down. "I'm not dressed. Hold on."

I left the door open and went to my closet. It was dark and I fumbled around, finally got the closet light on, which hurt my eyes. I found trousers, put them on, and when I returned Michelle was already inside and the door was closed. She leaned her back against it, left leg straight, right one crossed over it at the ankle, knee jutting forward, pulling her slacks tight, accentuating the shape of her thigh.

"I won't ask you for a drink," she said.

"Why not?"

"I want you sober." She stepped to me. Before I could think my hands moved on their own to her waist, held her lightly as if awaiting the start of dance music. Her lips mesmerized me; the perfect pale pink of them. I pulled her body into me and kissed her. Thanks to her long legs her narrow hard pubic bone found mine exactly while her breasts pushed against my breastbone. My cock hard now and her lips parted further so our kiss deepened. We made it to the bed and fell onto it. Her blouse was unbuttoned — had she done that or I? I pushed it back off her shoulders. She pulled her bra up, freeing her breasts to spill out. Then she swung a leg over me. The smell of her — of sex.

"I want you to fuck me good," she said. She reached back, grabbed my erection through my trousers.

"O'Malley . . . listen. How old are you?"

"What?"

"How old are you?"

"Why?"

She cupped one of her breasts, brought the nipple to my mouth. "Twenty-seven. Now suck me till I scream!"

"That's in this life?"

"What?"

"Twenty-seven in this life?"

She pushed my shirt up roughly and bit my nipple. "Are we going to talk or fuck?"

"Okay. But in your last life — how old were you in that one?"

"You're joking?"

"No. What I'm getting at — I wish you were younger."

She sat up. "You what?"

"Now — I wish you were nineteen."

She sat bolt upright, raised a hand and slapped my face hard.

"Ouch," I said. "Goddamn it!"

"Why not thirteen?" she spat.

"No, no, that's not what I mean. See, it would stop me."

"Stop you from what?"

"If you were nineteen you would remind me of someone I know, giving me the anti-aphrodisiac I need now to shut down."

"Why the goddamn hell do you want to shut down?"

"Because I have to."

She pulled her blouse tight to her, and held herself close, protectively. I had managed it: sexual inaction. A penis uninterested in performance. Michelle climbed off me.

"I'm sorry," I said. I rolled off the bed, stood.

From where she sat: "Some swordsman."

"I'm in a lose-lose. I don't do what you want and you hate me now. I do it and you hate me later."

"Why would I hate you later?"

"Because you'd want more of me than I can give."

She was off the bed now. "Goddamn men," she said.

"There, see what I mean?"

She stood, flushed with anger. "So what is it? Your lady friend — the doctor? She own you?"

"No," I said. "But I'm not just a fucking machine. Maybe I want more — sex with meaning."

She gave me a sour look. "Jesus, next thing you'll want is love."

After she was gone I lay back down, staring at the ceiling. It moved, vibrated, a shadow on it pulsing with an artery behind my right eye.

The bird dove toward me. It was coming for my eyes. I raised my hands and it careened by, its feathers brushing hard against the side of my head. I smelled death coming off it — sulfur and wet loam — as it turned away. It had missed! It climbed skyward again, accelerating. Something was wet on the side of my face. Blood? It circled fifty feet above me now, displaying its wide wings, taunting me. Its cold eyes on me, assessing me as prey. It dove again.

This time it would not miss.

Then I was airborne, flying above the falls, the crashing water below me. Was I dead? No. How had I survived? How freed my bound ankles? No clue.

I was mounted on something. Between my thighs, muscular shoulders. Outstretched behind me, huge wings. Extended in front of me, a long neck. The bird! I was riding it, mounted aloft, a passenger. Had I tamed it? Was it my friend? All was immensely silent, save the whistling of wind and the slow shuuush . . . shuuush . . . of wings beating the air.

We rose higher on an updraft, and I looked down again. Laid out below me, like a colorful map out of a children's book, the whole landscape of my childhood. Western New York state. Buffalo directly below, and southwestward, Lancaster, Hamburg, Fredonia, Jamestown. We started to descend.

I awakened abruptly. A ringing phone. I picked up the receiver. Wake-up call from the concierge's desk.

Twenty

My office as refuge; Mercedes advertising as a purpose in life, the purpose *of* life. Days passing methodically, relentlessly, the late autumn cold persisting. My New York consisted of my apartment, my office, a couple of midtown restaurants for expense-account lunches, and a couple of East Side haunts for late-night drinking. I avoided Grand Central Station.

All the while the machinery of resignation was working in me, the inner moving parts becoming focused to include what was desirable and exclude anything painful. A kind of stiffness invaded my gut, my veins, as if some mysterious inner organ secreted a fine liquid, forming, as it hardened, a protective barrier, a shell, such that all experience, impressions and ideas could penetrate only to it and no further. I could assess and react to selected stimuli mentally or physically. But my heart would be no part of it. There I would be safe. There I would not make the mistake again of venturing out, risking hard-won territory for imagined gain.

No more Minerva. No more Emily. I was resolved, and rock-hard in my resolution. If to survive demanded the old style — putting the past as far away as possible, focusing on the present and the immediate future — fine. I would be the old, reliable, tested Jack

Transit — an all-day performing machine with an appealing veneer.

But nights were a problem. I was not in control at night. Arriving home at eleven or twelve after dinner and drinks with colleagues, I'd collapse on my couch, the TV remote in one hand, a nightcap in the other, and feel the television sucking me toward it like some magician's box from another culture in which burned odd filaments of electronic witchcraft.

Then, head pounding and eyes narrowed and tight, to bed in hopes of sleep. But sleep not coming, and my mind jumping to life on its own accord, in a nightly round of sedition and self-attack, my thoughts circling me relentlessly, morphing from shape to shape. Always the outcome was this: I was alone in the world, alone by choice because alone was safe — except when it stopped being safe and became instead a dark hole into which I fell headlong, entering a deserted place devoid or air, light, sound. The aloneness could be dealt with only with tricks tried and true: competition with other men; ever-better performance at work; promise of more money. I drove my staff, drove myself, pushed the safety campaign; though at times I forgot why I ever committed to it (wondered if I ever knew). Forced belief in it because I must believe in something.

As for Mary, twice my hand was on the phone, awaiting my order to call. And I could not give it.

***

The cold Friday after Thanksgiving. Nine-thirty P.M. I stepped out of the cab, crossed the street to my apartment building. A man emerged from an alley. I'm suddenly hyperaware. I'm alone on the block, it's poorly lit, my doorman is in the lobby, out of sight and earshot. The man steps toward me. And I have a thought which I consider my life's exact low point: Good! Be a mugger. Come get me. And don't just rob me. Come kill what's left.

"Mr. Transit." High-pitched, familiar voice. He stepped out into the night-for-day effect of a distant streetlight's glow. Leather jacket, black knit gloves with fingertips cut away, long dark wool scarf, long black hair.

"Jeb?"

"Yeah."

"Christ, boy — scare the shit out of me."

"Sorry."

"What is it?"

"Minerva wanted me to come. Talk to you."

"What about?"

"She wants to see you."

I laughed, was both relieved and apprehensive. "Come on up."

"No, thanks."

"Well, what does she want?"

"To talk to you."

A glimmer of light, glimmer of hope; I'd given up, cursed not the darkness but the idea of light. But I did not trust hope. "I need more than that."

"Wants to have a heart-to-heart."

"We already did that."

"She's got more to say."

"About what?"

"Well . . . ." He exhaled. "I'd better let her explain. Can you come over tomorrow night? About eight-thirty. She'll make something. Dinner."

Turning this down held appeal. It would be the final acceptance of defeat. So I answered quickly. "Yes, okay."

He handed me a paper with an address. "See you then." He walked toward Central Park West. Upstairs, I poured a scotch, ran the shower. Dinner with my daughter. Light penetrates dark; icebergs melt as ocean water beneath them warms. And what of me? The ice in my heart?

***

At eight the next night, dressed in tan slacks, a cotton turtleneck, tan and red wool sweater and tan leather jacket, I arrived. In a bag, a bottle of California cabernet.

Their building presented an exposed brick side to Avenue B, displaying a spectacularly intricate graffito: BUZZ LOVES BRET in four-foot-high blue and yellow letters. I found Minerva's name and Jeb's above a mail slot, was buzzed in, climbed narrow, well-worn stairs to the fifth floor. The stairwell was clean and smelled of disinfectant.

Minerva was waiting for me at the open door. She wore threadbare jeans and a loose-fitting dark-blue top. "Hello," she said, and led me down a short hall into the small kitchen.

From the ceiling hung a dozen mobiles, intricate spidery constructs of metal, wood, leather, and fishline. I felt a blast of heat from the stove, where two cast-iron saucepans sat over lighted burners. The apartment was rich with the aromas of garlic, butter, and incense. The latter coming from a room, beyond a second doorway, which was hung with long strings of beads from lintel to floor.

"Great mobiles," I said.

"Thanks. I make them."

She picked up a spoon and peered under the cover of one of the saucepans. "I always steam vegetables too long. Think these are ready?"

"I'd say yes."

Jeb came through the hanging beads.

"Mr. Transit," he said, extending a hand. I shook it. He wore jeans with gaping holes at the knees, a T-shirt and leather vest. He led me into the living room, which was about eight feet by ten. A small couch, an ancient overstuffed chair, a couple of folding chairs. On a low table, a black boombox. Stacks of CDs. Posters of musicians on the walls, and a large piece of tie-dyed fabric, the shape of a jib sail, hanging from the ceiling, tacked there by its three corners. A small window looked out onto a fire escape. On the sill, a long stick of smoldering incense held erect in a tiny ceramic vase.

"Cozy," I said.

"Meaning small."

"Meaning well-tended. How long have you been here?"

"She was here. I moved in in March. Most stuff here is hers." Minerva came in with the cabernet and a corkscrew. Jeb did the uncorking while Minerva went out and returned with three wineglasses. Jeb poured.

"Thanks for coming," said Minerva. She held her glass toward me and we drank. "Wow, that's good. We're used to jug wine here." There was a moment of uncertainty. "Well, I think the food's ready. Come on." She led us back into the kitchen. A serving plate sat on a table, on it a carved roast chicken. Minerva handed me a plate and I served myself, then turned to the stove and spooned up vegetables from one saucepan and rice from another. Jeb followed, then Minerva, then we were back in the living room. I sat on the couch, balanced my plate on my knees, placed my wineglass on the floor. Jeb sat on a folding chair, Minerva on another.

"This is good," I said. "How'd you learn to cook?"

"Rebecca got me started, and I taught myself a little, too."

We ate. In the room, hanging in the air, an expectation of something to come.

"We play tonight," said Minerva.

"Really?"

She nodded. "Want to come?"

"Come hear you play?"

"Early gig — ten. Just one set."

"I'd like that."

I swirled the wine in my glass, raised the glass toward her. She raised hers in turn and we drank.

***

An hour later, we were in the backstage dressing room of a small club four blocks from the apartment. I sat on a stool, feeling alien and old; Minerva on a chair, across her knee a red electric guitar — a sleek, polished trapezoid inlaid with metal hardware. I watched the fingers of her left hand work on the frets, those of the right pluck the steel strings. She tuned the instrument carefully, bending her head low to a small amplifier, making adjustments in the volume knob and working the strings tighter or looser as she needed. She executed chords and phrases with effortless skill.

She had another electric guitar, a big black six-string Fender, and she tuned that one also. It had an angry, powerful profile and an aggressive, potent sound. Seeing it in her hands, yielding its power up to her, was daunting, nearly frightening.

After a few moments, two young men entered. One was hawk-nosed, intense, quick-moving, with long dirty-blond hair and a headband fashioned from a faded red cotton strip. He carried a big guitar case, wore denim jeans and jacket, and a T-shirt that said:

> HOWL TILL
> IT'S OVER

The other boy was shockingly young and had the wide, high-cheekboned face of a Native American. Brush cut, acne, red and orange cotton tights, knee-length flannel vest.

They kissed Minerva in turn. "Steel, Tommy, meet Jack," she said.

We shook hands. Steel, the one in the headband, took a huge white bass from his case and began tuning it, while Tommy rolled and lit a massive joint. Smelling marijuana again after many years was strange, comforting.

Minerva said to me: "You want earplugs?"

"Do I need them?"

Tommy coughed out a laugh, and Minerva reached into a drawer and handed me a pair.

"Condom for your ears," said Steel.

"Yeah," said Minerva. "Safe sounds, man."

Tommy, joint hanging from his mouth, said: "Ain't no such thing."

***

Minerva and The Avenue C Dysfunctional Band redefined the limits of sound for me that night. I stayed near the back of the club, looking over the heads of perhaps fifty kids, to where Jeb and Minerva on vocals, Minerva on lead guitar, Steel on bass, and Tommy on drums played arrhythmical, non-melodic, rage-filled, violent music. In a tiny space between the band and the audience kids danced.

Twenty minutes into the show, Jeb sang a hard-driving, dissonant song about a runaway child living in a Dumpster. Tommy had a drum solo, then Minerva played a really explosive series of riffs, and the place about came apart, kids bashing, moshing in the pit, throwing themselves into the air. I moved as far from that action as I could. I was angry at the violence of the music, at Minerva's contribution to it.

When it finally ended and people calmed down, Minerva said into the microphone: "Hey, okay, just for something different, this is for someone who's here tonight — and no laughing."

She began singing, a cappella, the old ballad: coming to San Francisco . . . gentle people . . . flowers . . . . The crowd was silent, confused; then boos and catcalls. Minerva ignored them. Her voice was raw and powerful, cutting against the sweetness of the lyrics, and it raised the hair on the back of my neck. The utter simplicity of this song, and more: its history as anthem of Emily's and my youth. As Minerva moved to the second verse, there was laughter, and the crowd grew louder in its disapproval.

"Hey!" Minerva screeched into the microphone, and the sound system squealed feedback, an electronic animal offended. Silence. "Like I said, assholes, this is for someone special. So shut the fuck up." I felt the sweet-sour of her tribute and her toughness; was attracted to her and repelled.

Among the audience, another kind of silence: sullen, tense, hostile. I thought: They'll charge the band before it's over. Minerva continued; lyrics of summertime, love and peace.

Nothing: no catcalls, no objections. She finished. A decided hush, polite applause, a few whistles.

"That was for my father, who's hearing me tonight for the first time, all right?" She motioned toward me; most of the crowd turned to see me. A few applauded. I blew her a kiss.

Twenty-one

*T*he set continued. The music became mellower, more melodic; or I became more accepting. By the time things wound down around eleven-thirty, I was hungry for more.

Backstage, Tommy was packing up his drums; Steel was helping him. Minerva's guitars were against the wall, but she wasn't there.

"How'd you like it?" Tommy asked.

"Wild." I shook his hand, and he bowed in a courtly way, then Steel came over and shook. He was soaked with sweat. Jeb stepped out of a bathroom, looking self-conscious.

"Hell of a show, Jeb."

"Thanks, man."

"Had me scared."

He grinned. "Oh, her number. Nah. They eat out of her hand."

"So where is she?"

"Changing." He inclined his head toward a door.

"You want to come, Jeb?" said Tommy.

"I guess."

"Where you headed?" I asked.

"Brooklyn. This band we know is playing out there, want to catch their late gig."

Minerva came in, toweling her hair. She'd changed into a sweatshirt and tights. Jeb and Minerva huddled, whispered. After a few moments, Jeb came over to me.

"I'm splitting with the guys," he said.

"Okay."

"This was, like, cool." He raised his hand, cupped toward me, and I clapped my hand into his. Jeb, Tommy and Steel left.

Minerva tended to her guitars, wiping them down as if they were alive. "You haven't said how you liked the show."

"I ended up loving it."

"For real?"

"Yes. You were fantastic," I said.

"Just okay."

"Your own toughest critic."

She nodded.

"Thanks for `San Francisco.´"

"Audience was a little weird about it," she said.

"I was moved by it."

She snapped the two guitar cases shut. We were alone in the room. She leaned against the wall, crossed her arms on her chest. "You said before that maybe we should make a plan for Emily."

It was a statement from another encounter, another world. It took me a moment to orient to it. "Yes?"

"You still want to?"

"Yes."

"As in what? A hospital? A place where she's safe?"

I nodded. She shifted her weight, spoke softly. "And you have the money?"

"Yes."

"Then maybe it might work."

I stared into her eyes; she met my gaze. "I thought she wouldn't go along with anything . . . any plan."

"There might be a way." She stepped away from the wall. "It means you convincing her."

From out in the club came voices and the scraping of chairs. I looked through the door, saw no one. "It's Vinnie, the owner," said Minerva. "Closing up. I know him, it's okay."

— 159 —

I sat on a stool, exhaled. Minerva continued standing. "See, I think she accepts you now. From that night. We can use that."

I waited, thinking. Then said: "What's made you change? You didn't want my help before."

A smile flickered across her lips, was gone. "Because by helping her, you'll help me. You take charge of her, I'm free."

"Free to . . . ."

"Go."

"San Francisco?"

She nodded.

"So I gain her and lose you." Immediately, a simple thought: *You can't lose what you never had.*

She looked away but not before I caught the distance in her eyes.

"No problem leaving New York?" I asked.

She spoke quietly, unrushed, unforced: "I want my life. New York is just pain to me. Pain and failure. They're everywhere. I hate playing rock. You didn't know that? And Jeb — he's a poet. He wants to write full time. Emily's gonna die here one day, but not me. How long have I taken care of her? Like forever. When do I get to live? You, you've got this life here, everything you want. You're like in another universe. Now's *my* time. I either grab it or miss it. You had that once, right? You grabbed for something. Took what you wanted, became what you wanted. I never had parents so I don't have anything behind me, just empty space. I've gotta have what's ahead, okay? Go for what I love."

"Which is what?"

She reached under the table and brought out a third guitar case, smaller than the others, worn and brown. She opened it and removed a Gibson acoustic guitar: blond rounded wooden shell, long straight neck, simple lines, gut strings. She held it by its neck, the unadorned, polished wood dull in the room's half light. Near the door was an old barstool with a torn plastic seat. She pulled it forward and sat, bowed over her instrument and tuned it.

"Bach composed for the lute, not the guitar, so it's all about transposition." I was two feet from her, could smell her hair and body, see perspiration at her hairline. "This is the Fugue in G Minor."

She just started, no fanfare, a natural progression from the tuning into the music. Elegant chords and hard, staccato notes. For a few moments I was without emotion, alert to how her hands moved, how her fingers found their places precisely on the frets. It was haunting, arousing music, and I tried to resist hooking up my feelings to it, as if that would be dangerous. Her playing was precise and intense, and I thought that in her posture she was looking for something within the music. After perhaps twenty bars she loosened up, looked away from her hands, right at me.

My breath got shallow at the impact of the music, and of her. Little by little I relaxed and the more I did the more the music begged me to feel. And the more I gave in, the fuzzier became boundaries between myself and her, between present and past. Minerva, Bach, guitar. Emily, Bach, flute. Small room now flooded with sound; small apartments then flooded with sound. Haight-Ashbury, New Orleans, Greenwich Village. Feeling beyond words; knowledge beyond rationality; the running flow of intuitive rightness, the fixed footing of inevitable relationship. And concepts made flesh: art, passion, continuity, family.

Out in the club, someone was sweeping up, and later a light went out, and harsh sirens blasted by outside, but Minerva played right on through them, the rigor and precision of her art stitching into the night a varied and votive offering. This music came from her, a product of mind and flesh and instrument, and she changed everything with it, and with her gift changed me back to something I once had been.

She finished. Echoes of chords. Silence. "So that's what I do."

There were no words I could trust. Finally: "You said before, not having parents, as you put it, there was only empty space behind you. That's how you feel?"

"Yes."

"May I be one now — a parent?"

Her expression was neither assent nor refusal. But it told me to continue.

"I've got an offer for you. I'll take over — take responsibility for Emily. Making you free to go west. But with a condition — that we stay in touch. We talk, write, whatever. But not just as a formality. That you let me in. Let me be your friend."

"Whatever that means."

"It means we trust each other."

"I'm not big on trust," she said.

"Neither am I, which will make it interesting."

"I always believed that you get the parents you deserve."

"No," I said. "Probably never."

She put the guitar into its case. "Will you come with me now to see her?"

"Meaning we have a deal?"

She nodded. A simple, eloquent gesture.

"Okay."

"But," she said, "it can't come directly from you — the news. You know?"

"Who then?"

"She only trusts one . . . person completely."

"You?"

"No." She stretched her arms out, moving them up and down to simulate wings.

We went out into the night. A light snow was falling, slanting down across tenements and streetlights, creating a fine scrim through which all was seen yet nothing was quite perceived as it really was. Buildings, cars, lights, walking people — all were softened and improved by the snow. I carried two guitar cases and Minerva one. We didn't speak but walked north to her place again, stowed the guitars inside, left, and walked west to the subway at Astor Place. Going down the stairs under the deco entrance cover we kicked snow from our shoes, the dull thudding echoing around us.

On the local train we stood on either side of the center pole. Minerva's hair was wet from melting snow, droplets forming, beading down her neck, glistening in the train's overhead light.

"Tell me something about you I don't know," she said.
"Such as?"
"Where you grew up."
"Jamestown, New York."
"Near . . . where?"
"Buffalo."
"What's it like?"
"Put it this way — it's not Buffalo you go to Buffalo for."
"What do you go for, then?"
"Niagara Falls."
"Come on."
"The boat — you go to see the boat. There's one out there, caught against some rocks, maybe a hundred feet from the lip of the falls. An old excursion boat, from the summer of 1910. Held twenty-five people, used for outings way upriver. This one time it got out into the surging part of the river, and broke away, and headed downriver toward the falls. People on the banks just watched in horror. It was heading for the falls, and then, when it was sure to go over, it got hung up on these rocks, and stopped. They rigged up this rope and pulley system — took them hours — and managed to save everyone. All the while hoping the boat wouldn't break free of the rocks and go over, which it didn't. Amazing part — my grandmother was on that boat. My mother's mother."

Minerva said: "Your grandmother?"

I like to think it hit us both at once. "Your great-grandmother."

"I never knew I had a great-grandmother. Or a grandmother."

"You almost didn't." A hint of humor in her eyes, plus something deeper — akin to wonder.

The train made local stops. At each station, more people getting on.

"You ever remarry after Emily?"
"No."
"There's a woman now?"
"Yes and no. I'm kind of on hold with someone."
"What's her name?"

"Mary."
"A professional?"
"Doctor."
"Why are you on hold?"
"She wants me to live with her."
"And you don't want to?"
"I don't know."
"You should do it," she said. "Live together."
"Why?"

The train went into a curve, its steel wheels screeching against the tracks. Minerva tried to speak over this, stopped. Finally it was quieter, and she said: "Maybe I'll tell you sometime. Meanwhile, we need a plan for when we see Emily. She can smell a lie from a hundred feet."

***

It was past midnight when we got to Grand Central. There were very few people there. Minerva led the way to the street and we turned north. From there, a doorway, stairs, another doorway. In five minutes, we were in an underground passage, went through a heavy metal door, descended another stairway which led to a sort of cul-de-sac formed by a curving brick wall. A huge duct ran across the ceiling at the height of eight feet. Light came from a single suspended bulb. In the wall the mortar was old and porous.

"Around here," said Minerva. She stepped through an opening at the edge of the wall. It was framed in wood, remnant of a door. I followed her. We were in a tiny unlit room with straw on the floor. It was warm and humid. A smell of damp cloth and sweat and something unhealthy I couldn't identify. At my elbow was a metal coatrack with clothes on hangers. Near us, a bedroll. Minerva knelt.

"Emily."

Movement in the bedroll. Emily's voice, muted: "Yes."

"Wake up."

"I was dreaming."

"Someone's here to see you."

Emily sat up. She was half out of the bedroll. Her face was puffy and her short hair looked nearly white in the poor light. She wore a gray sweatshirt.

"Who is it?" she asked.

"Jack," said Minerva.

"Tell him I don't need saving again."

"He knows that."

"What does he want?"

"To talk to you."

"I'm not what you call fit to be seen. Can't he wait?"

"He can wait outside if you want to get fixed up."

"A girl can't just be barged in on."

Minerva motioned me to leave, so I went back around the wall. I was nervous. This would be a one-shot presentation, no rehearsal, all the money on the table. Minerva came out for me. Emily was sitting up on her bedroll. She wore her cap again, had changed out of her sweatshirt into a blue flannel shirt. She smoked a cigarette.

"Hello, Emily."

"Bon soir."

"Sorry to wake you."

She nodded. She held the cigarette at chin level and the smoke rose lazily across her face.

"I've got news," I said, "but I don't know exactly how to tell you about it."

"Always the news man," she said. "You had news once; said you'd had it with poetry, it offered no kind of life. Said you were going to where they paid writers to write. Did you go there?"

I said nothing.

"I know you went there, wherever *there* is. What was it like? Streets paved with coins? Liquid gold running from faucets? Bare-breasted ladies wearing beaten copper backplates? Dollars flying in through airvents?"

She drew on her cigarette again, then touched the tip to a tin can at her knee that served as an ashtray. "As you can see my abode is lowly, my life a study in frugality. But you knew that. Have I thanked you?"

"For what?"

"For saving my hamhock last whenever it was. Did I tell you, M? There I was, naked in the ninth circle of Hades where devils are upside down in ice, and he came for me, this Galahad, this knight of the living order of Upper West Side yuppie-kings, and swept me up in the old tradition and brought me to a halfway house on a verdant plane, down below the gashouse."

She stopped, eyeing Minerva. "Of course I told you."

"Yes," said Minerva. "But listen. He's here for a different reason now, because something exciting has happened."

"What?"

"It's about Pegasus."

Emily lowered her cigarette.

"He's spoken again."

Emily's eyes narrowed and she looked from Minerva to me and back. "To whom?"

"To him."

Emily dropped the cigarette into the can, pushed up, stood. She wore a pair of soiled bluejeans and no shoes. She looked right into my face. Her eyes were bloodshot, and a vein was red and raised along the side of her nose. Her lower lip was cracked, lightly caked, as if medication had been applied and not wiped off.

"Tell me," she said.

"He says your time here is done," I said. "He wants something better for you now. He says it's time you're someplace comfortable, someplace safe. He's asked me to find you the right place. He knows this will make you happy."

Her face was a mosaic. Doubt, hope, suspicion.

"What else?"

"That you are to trust me. If you do that, he'll be waiting at the new place — your new home. The place I find for you. He'll be there."

Her face radiant, youthful; a study in hope. "Because he loves me?"

"Yes. He adores you."
"He always did."
"And always will."
"Because he's Daddy."
"Yes, because he's Daddy."

Her arms came up and around my neck. She hugged me, moved her face in toward me.

"You're not lying?" she whispered. Her grip was strong.

"Why would I lie?"

Her mouth was at my ear: "When you trashed poetry you trashed truth. You embraced the awful roiling place, the garden of deceit. I know that, you know it, the mayor knows it. So — do you have a sign from him, from Pegasus? Something to show he really spoke to you? That you're not spinning stories here?"

"He spoke to me. Gave me instructions for taking you out of here."

"Prove it."

I went blank. I looked at Minerva. She was intent, flushed. Too much time went by.

"Come on," said Emily. "Proof."

I hit on it. I could try, but it would require that Emily not remember how she confided in me in the cab coming back from All Angels Church.

"You don't have proof?" Emily's voice shrill, accusatory.

I took a breath. "He gave me a sign and some words." I tried to disengage her arms from me, but she was very strong. "Emily, let me go so I can show you the sign."

She dropped her arms. I stepped back through the doorway and rapped three times on the wooden frame.

She went still. "Oui?"

"Petite, tu es prêt?" I asked.

"Oui, mais qui es tu?"

"Moi, votre cheval."

Emily dropped to her knees, lowered her head. I joined her there, on my knees, and Minerva squatted beside me. Emily was weeping. I placed a hand on her shoulder.

"In a couple of days — two, three at the most — it will happen. Minerva and I will come here for you and take you to your new home. It will be a wonderful place with people who care. Warm, dry, clean. Good food."

"A safe place," said Minerva, "with a clean bed every night. They'll look after you. And he" — and she nodded at me — "will make sure you are happy."

"Why him?"

"Pegasus chose him."

"Why not you?"

Minerva went quiet.

Emily shrank a little, then intuition brought her to another place. I believe she knew that Minerva was leaving her. "I brought you into the world but not as a mother. I tried to tend you, but my sickness crashed into my brain, crowded me out; moved into my heart, blanked me out. You've been mother to *me*. Can you accept my love now, all busted up?"

Minerva's head dropped as if under a weight. "I've hated your sickness, and tried not to hate you. And that's worked. I have to have my life now, so Jack's the one to be strong."

Emily took this in and when she looked up there was slyness on her face. "Pegasus is the strong one," she said emphatically.

"Of course."

"He comes knocking, he decides, he looks after me."

"Yes."

"Right, Jack?"

Slyness and irony in her voice.

"Right."

Slyness and irony, and a touch of mockery: "He's behind it, he's spoken to you."

"Yes, exactly."

She lay down. She was calm, subdued. Minerva and I stood, prepared to go.

"So we'll come for you the day after tomorrow," said Minerva. Emily nodded. We backed out of the room. Suddenly Emily propped herself on her elbows, looked toward us.

"What?" asked Minerva.

"Truth is a net, catching falling things. Without it — smack! Ouch! Period."

On the way up to the street I asked: "Did she buy it?"

"She better have bought it!" said Minerva. Her voice quivering, her face a mask of desperation.

Twenty-two

The next morning I worked with Tom, firming up the work we'd outlined in Bucks County. At ten I excused myself, shut my office door, dialed my phone. Mary's receptionist answered.

"It's Jack Transit. Is she there?"

"She's with a patient."

"Could you have her call me? It's important."

She called in ten minutes. "Hello, Jack."

"I need your help. I have to get someone off the street. A sick person who's homeless. How do I do it?"

"You're calling me for this?"

"You're a doctor."

"How do I not feel . . . insulted? You were going to call me. When you were ready. Couldn't stand the thought of me being with another man — all that. That was two weeks ago. Christ!"

"You're right. I'm . . . out of line, inappropriate, whatever. Sorry." I felt I should hang up, and wondered if she would. Instead she asked, "It's Emily?"

"Yes."

"Is she cooperative?"

"Yes."

"Then it's easy. I don't have a clue why I'm doing this. I'll give you hospitals where you can use my name." She gave me three, and the head of psychiatric services in each. "Any one of them will do a good job of evaluating her. And the second two are excellent for long-term care."

"Thank you." I knew I was on extremely thin ice. "Listen, I've wanted to call but haven't been able to. Wouldn't let myself." Silence. "How are you?"

"Busy."

"When it's over with Emily, day after tomorrow, when I've got her where she has to be . . . I hope . . . know, I'm going to be in a better head. You have every reason not to see me, but I hope you will."

"Maybe, maybe not."

"Your . . . the guy . . ."

"Don't ask."

"Meaning he's not on the scene?"

"Meaning you're not entitled to know."

"Okay. Mary — thanks. I owe you."

I felt her wanting to say something. Waited.

"He's not on the scene."

"Good."

Within an hour I had made an appointment at Lenox Hill Hospital to bring Emily in two days.

***

Pete called before lunch. "Ready for another thrashing on the court?"

"Ooh, watch yourself."

"You up to it?"

"Name the time."

"Six tonight?"

"Grab a bite after?"

"You're on."

***

We finished storyboards and ads late in the afternoon, and I left them for Carl to look over in the morning. I went to the men's room and washed my face. Looked in the mirror. Made a point to remember what this feeling was like — for the next time I had to describe happiness.

On the squash court I stroked the ball like a twenty-five-year-old. I had a liquid coordination and a sharp, easy focus. We played two games, and I won 9 — 2 and 9 — 1.

In game three I was even smoother, freer, mind and muscles fully joined. To think was to move, and I chased down balls I hadn't been able to reach in months; I saw the ball into the racquet as big as a grapefruit, put the ball again and again exactly on the strings' sweet spot. My wrist was magically endowed with subtlety and my fingers with touch.

I hit a lot of drop shots, forcing Pete repeatedly to run up, then put his replies deep in the back corners, making him run diagonals and hit loose balls into the center of the court, and off these errant shots I placed tight drop shots again, so that I held the center of the court and watched him run. It was so easy.

After game five we toweled off and went to the drinking fountain behind the court.

"What's the deal?" said Pete. "You're playing incredibly well."

"I am in a zone."

"How'd you get there?"

"Luck."

"Liar," Pete said.

***

That night, dreaming:

> *I still rode the bird, and we descended now in slow circles. Below us was a grassy meadow and in its center one giant oak. As we lost altitude and neared it, I saw, in the fork of a branch, an enormous nest. It*

was wide and deep, and built from an inordinate number of twigs.

The bird hovered. I wanted very badly to land. The bird understood my wish and dropped, coming to rest on the nest's rim. Inside, it was smooth with dried mud, and very inviting.

I woke up.

***

Next day was the day. I would work in the morning, meet Minerva at noon, go for Emily.

At ten A.M. Carl appeared at my door, and I waved him in. He was grinning.

"How's your life?" he said. "Never mind, life doesn't interest me, advertising does. And right now I've got one word to say to you. Safety! Your safety hook for Mercedes. I saw the ads, the TV concepts. They represent — you ready? — a new level of maturity for this agency. I use that word carefully: it came to me this morning and I know exactly what the fuck it means. It means mature, as in grown up, worldly, responsible, the kind of advertising that will give us class we never dreamed of.

"So in short, I've flip-flopped totally. Ready? Playing the safety hook with Mercedes will blow the fucking Volvos back to Sweden, the Lexus back to Japan, show BMW up for what it is, a no-personality tinkertoy for gearheads. It's a bloody revelation, you walking genius, you knew it all along. But how did you know it? How did it hit you?"

"During a long look in the mirror."

He sat on a chair facing me, beads of perspiration on his high forehead.

"Very intriguing." He fished in his pocket for a cigar, found one, raised it like a baton, and my phone rang.

I waited for Irene to pick it up.

"Turns out," Carl continued, "I had a long talk with Donovan at Mercedes this morning, but without tipping our hand. I made it sound like a casual inquiry. Guess what? Mercedes has had extensive, sophisticated safety testing going on for forty years. Longer than anyone. And who knew?"

The phone was still ringing. My hand found the receiver and I plucked it off the cradle, held it.

"In Stuttgart, and here I'm quoting Donovan, they think of it as just something you do when you build the best car in the world. Never occurred to them to tell us about it; to use it, build on it, package it, make it sing. So you hit on it by instinct. Well, hat's off." He opened his mouth and carefully guided his cigar to the center, brought his teeth down on it, pulled matches from his pocket.

I raised a hand to him, and brought the receiver to my ear.

"Transit."

"It's Minerva."

"Hello."

"Emily. She's split again."

"What did you say?"

"Emily's taken off again, or is about to. I just heard about it."

The smell of cigar smoke enveloped me. Carl said, his voice mellowed by smoke: "Only thing we need to do to back it up is set up focus groups, just to be safe, no pun intended. One group of first-timers, a group of repeat buyers, probe this goddamn safety concept like we're looking for diamonds in a shit pile."

I put my hand over the receiver.

"Carl, excuse me." Back into the receiver: "What are you telling me?"

"The oracle. She sent one of her people with a message. Said Emily would kiss off Grand Central this morning, for good."

I stood, slapped my tabletop. "She can't do that! Christ!"

"I'm hoping I can stop her, so I'm going up there. Meanwhile, there's another riddle. I wrote it down."

"What do you think she'll do?"

"I don't know. I'm afraid what we said to her freaked her out. Like it didn't take."

"But it took, goddamn it! She was ready!"

"You want to hear the riddle?"

I sat, reached for a yellow pad, slapped it down in front of me, picked up a pen.

"Alright."

I wrote it down as she spoke it to me:

> Time matters. Follow your age minus three
> to the one square where all roads converge.
> At deux milles moins cinq see her,
> dead lust's child, not Bellerophon.
> And finally she's the shimmerer, quiet and spent.

I read it back to her. Then I asked, "Whose age?"

"What do you mean?"

"Whose age — who is the riddle intended for? We get that wrong we're fucked right up front."

"You. The messenger — the well-dressed man, the polite one — said, `this is for Mr. Transit.´"

"Okay." I shut my eyes to keep everything out — disappointment, anger, fear. But they all came right in anyway. I was trying to think, but emotion short-circuited logic, analysis. I waited a long five seconds.

"Okay, you get to the station. I'll try to decipher this thing. If I come up empty I'll meet you in the concourse."

I hung up. Carl eyed me. "Now what, Jack? Now what?"

"Emily," I said. "Just when I thought — "

I slammed the pad down on my desk and threw my pen across the room. "I'm back at the goddamn beginning!"

I took up another pen. My age minus three is forty-two. Follow it to the one square . . . easy, I take Forty-second Street to Times Square. Deux milles moins cinq — two thousand minus five — is nineteen ninety-five. An amount of money? An address?

Could be an address in Times Square. The rest was harder, but Bellerophon was familiar.

Carl was hovering, curious. I stood up.

"Where you going?"

"Gotta do something, Sorry." I tore the page from the pad, took my coat from the back of my door, hurried toward Tom's office. He was there.

"In mythology, what's dead lust?"

"What's *what*?"

"Dead lust. What does it mean?"

"No idea."

"Here, look at this." I showed him the riddle.

He said, "Our friend Bellerophon — "

"Who tamed Pegasus. And dead lust," I said. "You see?"

Tom scratched his head. "Drawing a blank on that."

"Grab your coat, come with me. I'll fill you in."

We headed to the elevator. Carl came along the corridor the other way, looking befuddled.

"Sorry, Carl," I said. "This thing just won't let up on me."

He walked us to the reception area.

"Life," said Carl. "It's a swamp, a plane wreck, a disease." He looked profoundly sad. "It's just a kick in the ass that it had to happen to you."

On the elevator Tom said: "So what's happening, exactly?"

"Emily's gone again. This is another riddle from the oracle."

His eyes got wide. Outside, we went to Forty-ninth and got a cab.

"You can trust this woman?" asked Tom. "The oracle?"

"She was right the first time."

"Which might have been luck."

The cab got caught in traffic between Fifth and Sixth.

"Come on!" I said. "Don't erode my faith now."

"Sorry."

"And you a classics man."

Tom mumbled something.

"What?"

"The classics are books," he said. "This is life."

"You up to helping me or not? Because if not, I can do it alone."

"No, no. I'll help."

The cab broke free of traffic, crossed Sixth.

"What do we do when . . . if we find her?" asked Tom.

"Get her straight to Lenox Hill Hospital. I'm checking her in." I held up the riddle. "I'm hoping the duex milles moins cinq is an address. Nineteen ninety-five."

"Let me see that," said Tom. "`Dead lust's child, not Bellerophon.´ Why not Bellerophon? *Who* isn't Bellerophon? And the shimmerer. What the hell is that?"

At Broadway we turned left, past Forty-sixth, Forty-fifth. I was looking at addresses. "Shit," I said. "We're too low. There's fifteen-fifty, fifteen-twenty."

"Let's see what's at Forty-third Street," said Tom.

We got out at that corner. Number 1501, the Paramount Building.

"Wait," said Tom, "I had a thought." He held up the riddle. "How'd you get this?"

"From my daughter."

"I mean how. How'd she convey it?"

"By phone. She read it to me."

"Okay, look . . . this . . . this." He fingered a line in the riddle. "`Dead lust.´ It could be an error in transmission. Listen to it, don't look at the words."

I didn't get it.

"Daedalus," said Tom. "It could be Daedalus."

"Daedalus' child," I said, "not Bellerophon. And Daedalus' child is?"

"Icarus. Who tried to fly and crashed to earth."

> At deux milles moins cinq see her,
> Daedalus' child, not Bellerophon . . . .

"Well," I said, "as long as we're revising, what if two thousand minus five means minus five hundred?"

"Equaling fifteen hundred?"

"Look." I pointed. At the corner of Forty-third and Broadway was a relatively new skyscraper. And on a black marble column near its door was its address: 1500.

Twenty-three

We crossed to 1500 Broadway. No sign of Emily. We went inside, up to the concierge at a large semicircular desk.

"We're looking for a homeless person," Tom said. "A woman —"

"You're what?"

"Do homeless people ever come in here? Have you seen a woman, a street person, plays a flute?"

"In here?"

"Yes, in the lobby, in the doorway . . . ."

"No sir. Over there maybe." He pointed toward the large windows facing the street. Through them I saw, across the street, a wall of shredded posters, graffiti, boarded windows. And hovering near them, four or five ragtag people. Three sitting huddled together, the others standing, talking.

Tom and I headed out, and crossed the street. They were street people alright, but Emily was not among them. I approached a large, bearded man in thick-lensed eyeglasses, wearing what looked like eight or ten layers of clothing.

"Excuse me, I'm looking for someone, a woman —"

He grinned. "Cherchez la femme."

"No, not that way. A woman — you know, homeless — named Emily, plays the flute. She's usually in Grand Central. Have you seen her here?"

"Nah," said the man. "Square One is Square One, a different crowd."

I stared a moment, then grabbed Tom's shoulder. "Christ! Square One. What's wrong with me?" I stepped into Broadway, arm up. A cab swerved over, and I hustled Tom inside it.

"Grand Central," I said to the cabbie. Then to Tom: "Square One is Grand Central. I *knew* that. We're on a wild-goose chase over here."

The cabbie, a small, narrow-shouldered man with a bushy head of reddish hair, leaned out of his window, shaking a hand at a panel truck. He yelled something at the truck driver, and traffic came to a halt all around us.

"So how do we explain fifteen hundred then?" asked Tom.

The Cabbie was growling, complaining. "I was supposed to be off at two-thirty," he said, "goin' home. Now look at me, stuck here."

"Buddy," I said, "get us to Grand Central, I'll pay you double the meter, then you go home."

He considered this. "I work twelve-hour shifts, when I go home I'm fucking tired, you know?"

I flashed on something. "What time is it?"

"Quarter of three," he said. "I been on the street since three A.M. I'm seein' double."

"Time matters!" I said to Tom. "Could it mean fifteen hundred hours? Three o'clock?" We both looked at the riddle.

> Time matters. Follow your age minus three
> to the one square where all roads converge.
> At deux milles moins cinq see her,
> dead lust's child, not Bell —

The cab lurched forward, throwing us back against the seat.

"Something's going to happen in Grand Central at three o'clock," I said. The cabbie swung us violently out into traffic and was past the truck. But traffic closed in ahead of us, the cabbie had to brake hard, and we stopped. I cracked a window, letting cold air in.

A second passed. "Chimera!" said Tom.

"What?"

"Here. Not `shimmerer´ — Chimera. I'm willing to bet. It's another tie-in to Pegasus. It was Bellerophon's biggest adventure. The Chimera was a deformed monster who guarded a mountain pass. No one could kill it, so Bellerophon attacked it from above, flew over it on Pegasus' back, shot down at it with arrows. He killed the Chimera."

I read: "`Daedalus´ child, not Bellerophon. And finally she's the Chimera, quiet and spent.'" I looked at Tom.

"First she's Icarus," he said, "trying to fly. Then she's the Chimera." He didn't go on, but I got it.

Death under a horse's belly.

In from my left temple, an incipient headache: a pinpoint of dread. I tapped the cabbie's shoulder. "Listen, drive on the goddamn sidewalk if you have to, but get us to the station in five minutes."

We moved, traffic cleared, we approached Forty-second Street, were halfway through the intersection. I yelled: "Turn left here."

"Can't — illegal," said the cabbie. "See the sign?"

"Fuck that! Make the goddamn turn!" I pulled my wallet out, thumbed in for bills. "I got — shit, what do you want? I got thirty bucks here — make the turn!" I threw money into the front seat.

But now pedestrians swarmed onto the crosswalk, a wall of people. The cabbie looked at me, shrugged.

"Fuck!" I said, opened the cab door, got out. "Come on," I shouted to Tom. He was slow in reacting. I started running. The long block to Sixth Avenue along the sidewalk, dodging people, running fast. After twenty strides Tom, close behind me, said, "I'm here. Go!" I removed my overcoat as I ran, clutched it in my right arm. At Sixth the light was with us, I ran across, keeping out of the crosswalk, clear of people. The block to Fifth had more stores so more people; progress was slower. We slowed to a quick walk in the thick crowd. Tom beside me, breathing heavily. We pushed through, resumed running. Crossed Fifth in a tangle of people. Hit the far sidewalk running. My lungs aching. I wanted to stop and walk, but refused to. Wanted to check my watch, did not; no point. Running was everything.

To the station doors, running through, down the long corridor, when I heard the music — soft, distant, high sweet strains — and we were running past the newsstand. Sprinting, I burst into the concourse, and . . . what was this crowd? Must have been a hundred people gathered in the large open section, everyone looking upward.

I did not want to look, did not want to see what they saw. But I did. There was Emily. High on the station's north wall are five enormous windows, with a white marble balustrade running the length of the station. She stood in front of the easternmost window, atop the balustrade, flute to her lips, head raised, playing.

The tune: "San Francisco."

But more than the playing, or her posture, or where she was, was what she wore: the ankle-length paisley wedding dress. And atop her head, her ancient wedding veil, which had been her mother's and grandmother's.

Tom stood beside me panting. "Where are the cops? They've gotta get her down."

But another voice got my attention; one I'll never forget. A high-pitched command, neither male nor female, young or old: "Jump!"

I looked up again, followed the poisoned arrow of this word to its target, saw that Emily heard it, saw her react. I moved further into the crowd, cupped my hands, yelled:

"Emily, get down from there."

Again, near me: "Hey lady, let's see you jump!"

I spotted him: a man in glasses, dark sweater, trimmed mustache, corduroy jacket. On his face a smile. He raised a cupped hand to his mouth, was about to shout again, but I got to him first and wrenched him by the forearm toward me. I got my other hand up between his shoulder blades and pushed. He went down on his hands and knees and I raised my right hand in a fist, had a spot picked out on the side of his face where I'd hit him. Before I could swing, the crowd gasped, and I looked up.

Emily had stopped playing and was stepping onto the balustrade railing. She walked it like a circus tightrope walker, her arms out for balance, the flute in her right hand.

"Emily, get down!" I yelled again, let go of the man, broke free of the crowd, and sprinted for the escalator. Pushing past people, I reached the top and ran forward, through a revolving door, where I nearly collided with Minerva.

"What's happening?"

I grabbed her arm. "Come on, come on." Back in the direction of the concourse were two glass doors on the other side of which was a balcony. I went through these doors, Minerva behind me. From down on the station floor came shouting, echoing, as if from another planet, another universe. Mixed into the sounds was a voice, louder than the others. I was sure it was Tom's: "Just stay there Emily. Just stay there, now."

I pivoted left, ran along the balcony, hoping, hoping — and yes! Two old doors stood half open. Beyond them a curved dark stairway going up. I led up one flight, two, then out onto a dank, dark open area, perhaps twenty feet by twenty. Three figures huddled in the far corner, one asleep on the floor, two sitting up. One — a pale, young face, thin, startled — looked at us. I ignored it, frantic to see where the stair continued. Past the three figures, a metal door stood open. I ran that way and we were going up another, narrower staircase. Close, air stale, my lungs now burning with effort. Minerva gasping for air behind me. This stairway seemed interminable, but at the distant top was a thin, vertical light. Approaching, I saw it was yet another door, open a crack.

I hit the door running, and it gave outward. Directly in front of me, the balustrade. Beyond it, above, dominating the ceiling, the huge face of Pegasus. And a few paces to the right, atop the white marble ledge, stood . . . my bride.

Her arms thin and bare, the cotton dress hanging on her slight frame: her wedding dress. From the crown of her head, trailing down her back, the fine lace veil. On her feet, tattered, frayed high-heeled black shoes.

There was a bizarre sound; distant babbling. It was the crowd below.

Minerva moved away from my side. I grabbed for Emily, but she scuttled away along the railing, and stopped, twelve feet from us, looking down. I took a step toward her.

She said, "Daddy?"

"Yes, Emily, it's Daddy. And I want you to step back down here to me."

She laughed a tinkling, girlish laugh. "No, Daddy," pointing up to Pegasus. "I'll come ride with you up *there*." I took another step.

"Anyway," she said, "you're Jack. Confess. You walked me up Rue Jacques Laffite, we did hash, made love, the river tide moving in, music in the square, bats in my head . . . ."

"Emily, come down now."

She shot a defiant look at me. Her eyes were blazing rounds of incandescence, burning into my face. "It's too late."

Minerva stepped around me. "Mother, come down, or I'll be angry with you."

Emily softened. "Minerva, ma petite. So pretty." She pointed to me. "You have *him* now."

She knelt, and with her left hand placed her flute on the railing. The scraping of metal on stone. She stood straight again. The heels of her shoes were worn down, and below the hem of her dress her ankles were thin, girlish. I pictured her thin calves, thin knees. I would grasp her there, by her knees, and ease her backward to sit on my shoulder. I stepped, was within six feet. All the rest was in slow motion: she bent her knees so her hem dropped to the balustrade, just touching. I stepped again as the hem edged upward, a curtain teasingly raised. Her ankles lengthened and her heels elevated, revealing the soles of her shoes. In the left sole was a ragged hole plugged with a wad of newspaper. Only her toes now touched the balustrade, then nothing was touching. I lunged for her. She jumped high. My heart leapt with her, all but exploded. She floated in space. Above her, her veil spread out creating a lace canopy. For a long instant it became a sheer, floating overlay to what was directly above: Pegasus' head and body. She had joined perfectly his white, unmoving wings.

Twenty-four

I drove through the tall cemetery gate and up a narrow road guarded by leafless oaks and maples — hibernating giants saluting the sky. Ahead, cold noon sunlight slanted toward us across the headstones. Minerva sat beside me in the car, arms folded, a single red rose across her lap. We crested a hill, and I saw the hearse parked on the road. Two black-clad men stood near it, smoking. I parked behind the hearse, and Minerva and I got out. On a rise across thirty feet of dormant brown grass and scattered fallen leaves, the casket sat on a support above a dug grave. It looked very small. We stood waiting. Along the road came Jeb on his Harley, in helmet and cycle leathers. He parked behind the car, removed the helmet, hung it on a stainless-steel backrest behind the seat. He walked to Minerva and me, and we three went up the hill toward the casket.

We were halfway there when I heard a banging and backfiring down on the road and turned to see a strange car approaching — a dented and rusted twenty-year-old Volkswagen Thing. It had a ragged convertible top and no windows. It parked and the Grand Central Four emerged: Marvin, whom at first I did not recognize; Burt, whose nose was bandaged; the well-dressed man, who wore a blue suit, a skinny knit tie and overcoat; and Mrs. Jenkins, who had changed from her sweatshirt into a knit sweater and ankle-length wool skirt and cloth jacket. Marvin waved, and led the others up the hill toward us. Under his arm he carried a shoe box. His hair was black and he wore it in a brushcut.

I shook his hand. "I had to look twice. Where's your turban?"

"What turban?" he asked.

Burt caught my eye and winked.

Marvin said: "Looks like we're not late. I was worried. We were pursued. Phalanx of state police, helicopter, Bradley fighting vehicle. Had to take back roads to lose them."

We all went on up the hill. Our feet crunched on the frozen grass. The casket was shiny aluminum. We stood looking at it in silence. I pictured Emily in there, her broken body laid into a satin bed.

Minerva was pale, and I took her hand. Burt had a hand over his face, and Mrs. Jenkins stared at the sky.

Marvin leaned to me. "The good news is she's got work."

I gave him a look.

"Oh, yeah — nice gig in New Mexico. They always loved her there." He waited another moment. "May we?"

I nodded, and he and his group stepped to the lip of the grave. He opened the shoe box, and something metallic fell from it and clinked to the ground. Marvin picked it up, passed it to the others, each held it a second, passed it on. Finally, Marvin dropped it into the grave. They continued standing awhile, then Burt broke ranks and moved away. As he passed me, he reached out a hand and we shook. The well-dressed man followed him, nodding. Mrs. Jenkins came next. She didn't look at me but moved quickly past. For some reason I glanced down at her feet. She was wearing running shoes, and the toe of the right one was badly scuffed. I'd seen that shoe before, remembered where. Shocked, I watched her descend the hill. Marvin was still at the grave.

"Tell me about Mrs. Jenkins," I said.

He was mute.

"It's her, isn't it — the oracle?" He was noncommittal. "Goddamn it. She knew Emily was going to kill herself. And she did nothing."

"She did a lot. It's not her job to change fate. Only to enlighten."

"Then now's her chance to enlighten me!" I said angrily. I hurried down the hill after her. She was crossing the road toward the battered car when I caught her.

"Wait!" I said. She faced me calmly. Wizened, puckish face, too many wrinkles, too few teeth, eyes deep-set under hairless brows. "I've got an issue with you."

"Okay."

"You knew Emily was going to kill herself. Why'd you let her?"

"Here's a question for you that requires an answer that is entirely honest. Would you want her alive now?"

"Yes!"

"Why?"

"Why not?"

"No, no. *Why?*"

"First, she deserved to live. Second, she could have been cured."

"First, none of us know who deserves to live. Second, impossible."

I bumped her. It was a sort of body push, born of extreme anger. "How do you know? Are you God?"

"No, nor are you. My case is this: her life was over in her mind. And she attained her second-strongest wish — that Minerva be free of her. This parallels your need — to be free of Emily also. Which you now are, and with a somewhat clear conscience. You look skeptical, so here's my third question to you: if you could go to that casket now and touch it and revive her exactly as she was, would you do it?"

"Yes."

"It would be a selfish act."

This stung, and silenced me. After a moment I said, "If freeing Minerva was Emily's second-strongest wish, what was her strongest?"

"Getting free herself, which, in her mind, only Pegasus could accomplish."

"Or her father."

"One and the same."

My anger had leached out of me, and in its place a final burning question. It humbled me to ask it. "Did I cause Emily's suffering?"

"*Did* you?"

"No! If I'd never been born, she would have suffered as much."

"Or more." She did an odd thing then — she curtsied. Then stepped to the car. I watched her get in, stood alone in the road. This is how revelation comes? From an old woman in worn sneakers, riding in a Volkswagen Thing?

I stepped back to the grass. Just in from the road was a lone oak, denuded in the December cold. I heard a rustling and a twig fell past me. I looked up. A bird perched atop the tree. A robin off its seasonal schedule, or a kestrel, hunting. It was looking down at me.

I trudged back to the gravesite. Marvin was still there, along with Minerva and Jeb. I joined them and looked into the grave. Lying at the bottom, shiny and silver in the black dirt, was the mouthpiece of a flute.

"She can scam an instrument in Taos," said Marvin, "no problem. But a mouthpiece . . . that's personal. She'll want her own. Gotta look after her interests."

I put my hand on his shoulder. "You were her great friend."

"Not so great," he said.

"You loved her."

"Someone had to."

Moments passed and he said: "You're family, you'll want to be alone here."

Below, the car clattered to life, the engine sounding like metal at serious war with metal.

"Oh," said Marvin, taking a credit card from his pocket and handing it to me. "We don't need this anymore. What we needed was wheels — now we got 'em. Thanks."

I took the card. Marvin walked down the hill. Minerva, Jeb and I watched him get into the car, which rattled off.

Everything was immensely still. The casket reflected sunlight. Minerva placed her rose on it. The flower's intense, vibrant redness was set off shockingly by the aluminum casket top, the brown deadness of the grass, the yellow and brown deadness of the leaves, the dark earth of the grave.

Minerva said: "Bye, Mother."

She took my hand again and we stood a long moment. She let her head rest lightly on my shoulder, and I slipped my arm around hers. Jeb held her other hand. Finally, I scooped up a handful of dirt, held it over the grave, let it sift slowly between my fingers: a dark shower of earth. It fell as I intended, onto the mouthpiece.

I said: "Au revoir, Emily. Have a great show in Taos."

We went down the hill. I walked slowly because of what was next. Once back on the road we stood silently near Jeb's bike. I thought I'd prepared for it, but I hadn't. Minerva took my hand.

"It has to be now," she said. I nodded. She looked at the sky. "Jesus, will it ever warm up?"

"You'll take the southern route, I hope?"

Jeb nodded. "Down to Virginia, across Tennessee, pick up some of old Route 66, Oklahoma, Texas panhandle, New Mexico, up to L.A., on up the coast, like that."

Minerva was bent over the bike, her hand in the rear saddlebag. She turned and held Emily's flute case out to me. I saw it, but didn't; didn't see what it meant.

"For you," she said.

An awful finality awaited the act of taking it, which I did not want, so instead I opened the catches and raised the top. Emily's disassembled flute lay there, deep in its threadbare bed. I touched it, slowly running a finger from end to end, over the keys, which were cold. One piece was missing — the mouthpiece. I closed the case, snapped it shut. And there, on the top, the tarnished bronze plaque with her name joined forever with my own.

Still I hesitated. Minerva said: "Go on, you should have it." I took the case which was light in my hands, and small, and worn smooth with years. Feeling hit me then. I let go, Minerva moved to me, and her arms were around my neck. We stayed this way awhile, then she pulled back a little, but my emotion stayed strong. The taste of salt was on my lips.

Tears.

Minerva's eyes were on me. *Yes, see me, Minerva. See your father in his loss. See what he is, now that he can love.*

Ten seconds passed — a lifetime when you grieve and try to stop grieving. Finally Jeb swung a leg over the Harley, put his foot on the kick starter.

Minerva was looking at me in a peculiar way. "Remember how I said I thought you should hook up with your lady — Mary?"

"Of course."

"And that I had a reason?"

"Yes."

"Well, does a baby come into it?"

I didn't follow.

"Will she want to have one?"

"Oh. Yes."

"So do it."

I checked her eyes for irony. None.

"You'd make a good father."

I went blank. Her hand was up: I thought she was going to brush something off my face, or my hair, but instead she touched me, lightly, on the cheek. Those eyes, gray, intense with knowledge attained early and held deeply, held me fast. I wished to reply, and had the words, but had to work to find the voice behind them.

"Thank you."

Jeb pushed his foot down hard, and the motorcycle roared to life.

Minerva mounted up. I moved closer to them to be heard. "Wait. Remember our deal?"

"Yes."

"We're . . . connected now."

"Yes."

"Meaning letters, cards, a call. But I don't have your address."

"I'll send one," said Minerva. "Meantime, care of the Music Conservatory, San Francisco. Trust me."

"I'm not big on trust."

She got it; she remembered. And her laugh was perfect.

"So study well, and get ready for a visitor. In the spring, maybe?"

Minerva nodded. Jeb engaged first gear, and the bike moved away, wheels crunching gravel. I watched their backs, Minerva's long, leather-clad legs astride the bike, an arm around Jeb's waist. She looked back and waved, I waved, and they moved along the road, which dipped down. I stepped up onto the bank to keep them in view. Then they were gone except for the sound, which echoed off a far hill.

I was standing near the oak again and felt something under my foot. There on the ground was a tiny pile of twigs, round and symmetrical. I knelt. It was a decaying bird's nest, six inches in diameter. The nest must have fallen and lain just there since the summer, rotting at a slow pace. The mud that had been its adhering interior was white-gray and crumbly. Neatly in the center was a tiny bird's skeleton, absent skin and feathers. Just next to it, touching the bony architecture of what would have been the chick's wing, lay a fragment of eggshell, still palely blue against the dark twigs.

I stood, peered up at the tree. The bird was still there. It jerked its head once, bolted, and flew. I clasped Emily's flute case tightly under my arm, walked toward the car. The bird was gone from sight.

It's good at that. Its life is flight, and forgetting is bred into its bones.

"Not me," I said aloud. "That is not me."